Alabaster Dangermond
and the Serpent's Blade

Alabaster Dangermond and the Serpent's Blade

By Jason VanHorn

Book 1 in the Dangermond Series

Isaac,

Enjoy All!

Goldenwood Press
Grand Rapids

ISBN 978-09996034-0-6 (paperback)
ISBN 978-0-9996034-1-3 (ebook)
ISBN 978-0-9996034-2-0 (Kindle)

Cover Art and Logo Design by Scott Harshbarger of The Art of Harsh, www.theartofharsh.com, @theartofharsh on Instagram.

First Printing January 2018

Published by Goldenwood Press LLC
Grand Rapids, Michigan

For inquires, please contact the editor at goldenwoodpress.com

To learn more about amazing books already in print or upcoming, please check out goldenwoodpress.com & alabasterdangermond.com

For Isaiah, Nathanael,
Eleanor, & Luke

Type in all the coordinate locations mentioned in this book in the special online interactive map when you visit alabasterdangermond.com

Also, look for the secretcode hidden in the text of this book. Find the 10 special **bold** letters and type them in order into the SECRET ENTRANCE on alabasterdangermond.com

1

Death Descent

LONG ISLAND, NEW YORK : PRESENT DAY
40.728854 N, 73.118033 W

Alabaster Dangermond blew a kiss into the air to honor his dead parents and then fell into the abandoned elevator shaft.

Watching floor after floor zoom past, the fourteen-year-old looked down toward the bottom. It was deep and the dark was coming. In less than 20 seconds, it would be over. The illuminated shaft would soon turn pitch black and then Al would be blinded by the darkness. Falling fast, he saw blurry large numbers painted in black on the concrete walls. It smelled like wood paneling. Al thought it was probably from all the woodwork in the five-story New York mansion.

Seeing the large zero on the wall whip past, the teenager entered the darkness below the mansion. The dark was more dangerous than the light. One small adjustment to the left or the right in the free-fall and he would go skipping off the side, crushing his five and a half foot frame, or worse, his head. It was nothing like skydiving.

Skydivers angle themselves in free-fall to slow or speed up as air pushes against their body. They choose when to deploy their lifeline of a parachute to take them gently back to the earth. In the dark vertical tunnel, Alabaster had no backpack clinging to his body and no parachute would save him today. He used to wear a helmet in the shaft, but now he dropped with only the black outfit on his body and his mussy blond hair standing on end.

Al had rediscovered the shaft a couple of years ago after finding the original plans to the house. First dug to lead to a secret underground headquarters deep in the ground, the project was abandoned because the rock was too hard at the bottom.

Before he started regularly jumping in the shaft, he measured the distance from the top to the bottom. The amount of rope he had to tie together just to get to the lowest part of the shaft was ridiculous. It took eight delivery trucks packed with boxes of braided rope to get him the entire order. It was so preposterous that anyone would need that amount of rope, the company called him three times just to confirm that he actually wanted that many boxes delivered. Even though there were other means to measure the distance, Al wanted the rope. He even convinced his best friend, Turnkey, to join him latching the ropes together end to end. In total, the elevator shaft was about 1200 feet deep. After the measurement, the braids found a home as part of an intensive ropes-training course stretched among the trees on the extensive mansion grounds—with the Chief's permission, of course. Once it had been measured, he and Turnkey started jumping down the shaft.

Swallowed by the dark, Al began to count in his head, listening to the rushing air zoom past his ears. Reaching down to the holster on his hip, Al pulled out his favorite pistol. Lifting it up in front of him, he grasped it with both hands. The force of the air made it difficult to keep his arms steady. Adjusting slightly higher, he pulled the trigger in the dark.

Out of the end of the pistol, a small blue flame burst as the special bullet moved at 2500 feet per second, hitting the concrete wall in the 15-foot wide shaft almost instantaneously. The area exploded with streaks of blue light up and down the walls, giving Al a glimpse of the whole shaft as it flashed before his eyes.

"Did I get it?" Al asked loudly as he holstered his Electro-pistol.

"So close, yo! Off by four inches according to sensors," Turnkey said in Al's earpiece.

Al had been trying to hit the target he placed in the shaft months earlier. It was not much bigger than a quarter on the wall and every time he plunged, he tried to shoot that hidden spot, masked by the dark. He improved all the time, but he never hit it.

Dampness filled his nose, which meant the end was near. The first time he attempted this fall, his heart had pumped hard in his chest. Now with 57 jumps under his belt, he relaxed his body to feel the force of the air.

"Imminent ground," he heard spoken into his ear. Immediately he put his hands in front of him close to his face. All around his body, a large gel pillow instantly deployed from his black suit, surrounding him and stopping his fall. He reached the bottom of the elevator shaft. Yet again, one of Mary-Anne's inventions had saved him. Completely encased, Al couldn't move as he stared forward through the translucent plastic. The small pocket of air in front of his face, formed by putting his hands on his head so the gel pillow wouldn't suffocate him, gave him enough air for a minute before the gel would eat through the plastic pillow and then evaporate off, leaving no trace.

Mary-Anne had designed and constructed the Impact Suit and handheld Electro-pistol in her laboratory. Weapons were her particular specialty and Alabaster always had the best time testing her unique creations. The care she gave to each of the inventions she created showed her passionate ingenuity and genius. Turnkey always said she was the coolest girl he had ever met, and every time Alabaster used one of her gadgets, he thought so too.

The lights at the bottom of the shaft cranked on, illuminating the entire area. On the walls of the hollowed-out rock were the letters U.S.A.—the Undercover Secret Agency. Al could see Turnkey and Mary-Anne through the gel pillow. His tall dark-skinned friend towered over the short girl with brown hair. As they approached, the gel pillow began to deflate and disintegrate around him.

Fourteen-year-old Turnkey put out his fist for a bump. "Bro, that was slamm'n! You almost hit the target."

Mary-Anne smiled. "Yeah, Al, that was close. Next time, you'll probably get it."

"Man, just four inches," Al said as the last of the plastic fell to the ground and disappeared. "Your Impact Suit is amazing as usual, Mary-Anne."

The short thirteen-year-old girl fidgeted. "Thanks, Al."

Al ran a hand through his hair. "Well, I'm glad your computer A.I. can sense when I'm going to hit the ground. Otherwise…well, it wouldn't be a pretty—"

"Attention. Attention. All Junior Agents report immediately to Briefing Room Two," the voice blared over the speaker in the room. All three Junior Agents covered their ears as they moved toward the elevator—the echo from the underground rock was brutal.

Turnkey looked at his watch. "Aww, man, it looks like we are going to be late again, yo. This elevator is so slow."

Mary-Anne nodded. "Al. What number are you at?"

Al looked down at his computer watch and accessed his attendance. "Ten. The Chief said if I hit ten, he was going to kick me out of the academy. I guess we shouldn't have practiced our jumps this morning."

Turnkey looked at Al. "Yo, he'll let you off, homie. You have a good reason. This brief wasn't planned."

"I doubt it, TK. I think the Chief has it out for me—he's always so hard on me. This will just give him the ammo he needs to send me packing."

Alabaster Dangermond hoped the Chief would have

mercy, but he knew the man too well. He was all out of chances. Al began to feel sick to his stomach. This was his last day as a secret agent.

2

The Chief

Out of breath, the three Junior Agents pushed through the door to Briefing Room Two.

The room was full of mahogany panels with a large table in the center. Sunlight from the outside poured through the tall windows. There were seven Junior Agents already around the table. The glare from the Chief made Al look away. The large-bellied man always wore a dark suit—Al thought the color went well with the Chief's personality.

Mary-Anne was easily the most liked among the three and, as the most talented, the guys always counted on her to smooth things over when they were in a jam.

She spoke first, "Sorry, we're late, sir—"

"I don't want to hear excuses, Ms. Martinez. Sit down, you three, and be quiet," the Chief said.

With all the comfortable cushioned seats taken by other Junior Agents, Al and his friends found some hard wooden chairs to sit on against the wall. Sweat poured from Al and Turnkey's foreheads as they took their seats. If anyone would have guessed, they might have said the boys had just come off the basketball court.

"As I was saying," the Chief continued, "In a few days, the Central Intelligence Agency will take over my Agent Trials. I recognize this is a new approach and that notification is late. Nevertheless, I have agreed. Normally, at fourteen, you would be ready for promotion from Junior to Assistant Agent in the Undercover Secret Agency by passing my tests, and then you'd head to Washington when you turned sixteen. But the CIA said they will take those that pass their version of the Agent Trials straight into their ranks. If promoted, you will move to Langley Headquarters outside of Washington, D.C., and begin your new training assignment there. Anyone younger than fourteen will not participate in the Agent Trials and will remain here." The Chief looked directly at Mary-Anne. She was the only Junior Agent in the room younger than fourteen.

A tickle tugged at Al's throat. He coughed.

The Chief looked over to where Al sat. "You've been training since your admittance into the U.S.A. and I expect you will all pass with—"

Al couldn't stop coughing. His eyes began to water.

"What in heaven's name is wrong with you? Get ahold of yourself, Agent Dangermond!"

Sweat cascaded down Al's face as he looked across the room at the pitcher of water beyond the Chief in the corner, incessantly coughing.

Turnkey motioned with his hand. "Sir—"

"No! No excuses. Agent Keystone, just get the boy some water."

Turnkey got him some water and Al downed it to soothe his parched throat. When Al chugged the last bit of water, he realized everyone in the room was staring at him. Mary-Anne fidgeted on her chair.

"Right. Well, now that Agent Dangermond is through, perhaps I can continue?" The Chief looked directly at Alabaster. Al knew better than to say anything. Everyone in the room adjusted their focus back to the front.

"I expect all of you to pass the Agent Trials. They are meant to be hard, but you've been in training since your ninth birthday and there is no reason the Trials designed by the CIA will be any different than the ones I've designed. All of you displayed excellence in your sports activities with the Universal Sports Academy and that is why I recruited you here into the U.S.A. You have strong signs of physical strength and agility, but it is your mind and your mental toughness that will give you success as agents. Are there any questions?"

The Junior Agents looked around at each other. Smirks appeared on a few faces but the room remained silent.

"That will be all, then," the Chief said. "Except for you, Mr. Dangermond."

Al watched the cohort of Junior Agents stream out of the room. Turnkey and Mary-Anne got up and tried to give Al a reassuring smile, but quickly turned their attention back to the Chief when he spoke.

"Agents Keystone and Martinez. I expect better from

you both. Each of you will receive a demerit for being late. Don't let it happen again."

"Yes, sir."

As Mary-Anne Martinez walked by, she put her hand on Al's shoulder and gave him a short nod. He could always count on her for encouragement. Al looked over to his best friend and they locked eyes as Turnkey exited the room after Mary-Anne. Al desperately wanted to follow his best friend as the large wooden door came shut.

The end had finally come.

Al needed another glass of water but his arms and legs wouldn't move from their spot. Like pieces of metal near a large magnet, the attraction to his chair was overwhelming. His affixed position on the wooden chair became even more uncomfortable as the large man came closer. He thought the Chief wasn't so bad, but he hated a scolding. Every time he got in trouble, he was reminded of his parents. He missed them so much. Long dead now, he wondered if they would have been like the Chief. He always came to the same conclusion.

Al hung his head. "I'm sorry, Chief. I know my parents put you in charge of me and you're just looking out for me."

The big man sighed. "Alabaster, I have no room for softness. I expect you to live up to your potential. When you are late to meetings, you put me in a difficult position. I do not have the luxury of giving you special treatment among the other Junior Agents just because I am your guardian. I'm still the boss of this agency."

Al knew it was coming. His career as an agent was about

to end before he even had a chance to prove himself. His parents first enrolled him in the Universal Sports Academy boarding school when he was five years old. Two years later when his parents died, Al stopped competition climbing altogether, but the Chief kept him enrolled in the academy.

The sports academy had a reputation of producing Olympic champions and strings of professional athletes in many sports. Admitted students entered a dual program in sports and education curriculum. And for some who had high scores in certain sports and school subjects, a special offer was made. A clandestine program of the sports academy existed called the Undercover Secret Agency, or the U.S.A., and Al had taken the secret exams to enter when he was nine.

The Agency was set up as a prep-school to produce secret agents for the CIA. Graduates of the Undercover Secret Agency usually entered the CIA when they were sixteen. Now he had a shot at entering early if he could pass the Agent Trials. Studying to become a CIA Agent had become his sole purpose in life since the time he entered the program. It was everything he wanted. But the boss had leveled his threats for tardiness. Now it was the end.

"Agent Dangermond."

"Yes, sir."

"You will report to Mr. Underwood, our mansion custodian, for one week to clean and prepare every room he assigns. You, of all agents here, have the best grasp on timing. Your free falls down the abandoned shaft help you work on your timing and precision, do they not? Yet, you can't seem to find the ability to make it to briefing meetings on time."

"So, I'm not kicked out of the program for my tardiness?"

"Kicked out? No. I've changed my mind about that. You will learn more lessons through this punishment than if I kicked you out. Consider this punishment part of your training and learn from it. Underwood is going to push you hard. Furthermore, I'm going to activate the Vitals Tracker chip in your shoulder to keep tabs on you. It will tell me exactly where you are at all times. I'm going to authorize Underwood to access it as well, so he can know where you are according to the room-to-room cleaning schedule he will give you. Alabaster, I am sure your parents would expect better of you, if they were still with us."

Al sighed deeply. There was nothing he missed more than his parents. A day never passed that he didn't think of them. Apart from the few pictures he owned, he'd forgotten so many things already. Their hugs. Their smiles. Even their smell. All Alabaster had left of his parents was some money they gave him in a trust and the large man in front of him assigned to be his guardian.

"I understand, sir. I'll go see Mr. Underwood," Al said as he looked down at the floor.

The Chief spoke softer, "Alabaster. You are one of the finest students here at the agency and good at many things. Just pay better attention and keep trying to improve and one day you will make a fine agent."

At least the Chief wasn't completely heartless. There was a ray of hope somewhere in what he said.

"Sir. One last thing. Do I still get the chance to participate in the Agent Trials?"

The big man came close and even though he was so large, he got down on one knee next to Al. The teenager had never seen him do this before.

"Of course you are going through the Agent Trials. I expect to hear a good report on you. Remember to focus your attention and you will be fine."

Al could almost feel the rays dance on his skin, as sunlight bathed the room. "Thanks, Chief."

"Now, go report to Mr. Underwood. You have a lot of cleaning work to do for him."

Al got up from the chair and walked toward the door. As he did, he felt his wrist vibrate.

Looking down at the watch that Mary-Anne had designed, he saw he had a new email message:

> To: aldangermond17@unisportacademy.edu
> From: ZM@blg.ml.si.com
> Subject: Your Parents' Death – For Your
> Eyes Only

3

Cold-Blooded Murder

Al felt a rush of adrenaline course through his veins as he stepped into the wood-paneled hallway of the huge mansion. Turnkey and Mary-Anne were waiting for him.

"Al! What happened?" Mary-Anne asked.

"What? Huh? Oh," he mumbled looking up and down at his friends and his watch.

"Yo, man, what happened with the Chief? Are you staying here?"

"Uh, yeah, TK. He let me stay. Hey. Can you give me a minute? I just got this email from someone and I need to check it."

"Yeah, sure, homie. Me and Mary-Anne are heading outside. She wants to teach me some new things in tennis. You gonna join us?"

Mary-Anne smiled at both of them.

Al kept looking at his watch. "Uh, yeah. Just let me check on this and I'll come find you two. Cool?"

"Sure, man." Turnkey and Mary-Anne headed down a different hallway toward the tennis courts outside.

Al moved over to a corner bench in the hallway and sat down. Looking at his watch, he opened the email:

> Greetings Alabaster,
>
> Your parents had something to say and I've attached a short video clip for you to enjoy. Sorry it doesn't have any sound, but that was the best I could do. If you show anyone, I will kill you and your precious friends, starting with Turnkey. I know who you are and what you do at that school.
>
> Sincerely, ZM

ZM? Who is that? There was an attached video file. Alabaster clicked the file and the video played on his watch screen. He moved over to a corner in the hall where it was a little darker so he could see it better.

Al's stomach flipped over as he watched his mom and dad get pushed through a door into a room with glass walls. The camera angle was looking down obliquely from a corner inside the glass room. In the lower left corner of the video, a timestamp was dated September 24th, seven years ago. There was no audio stream, just video.

But they died in a car wreck on June 1st of that year. How could they have been alive after they died?

Al could make out a table in the room with a contraption on top of it. As he watched, his shoulders tightened. Both his parents, Thomas and Cynthia Dangermond, stared at the table and then he saw a timer switch on. The camera angle zoomed closer and he could see it was a bomb with a countdown timer. Al's throat tightened and he swallowed hard.

Three minutes to go.

His mom turned and looked up as if someone were talking to them. Then she turned and looked at the device. It had four tubes of liquid attached to a black box.

She turned and yelled something but Alabaster couldn't make out what it was. It was hard to follow without sound.

He saw his parents work quickly to get the main panel off. His mom looked at his dad, but he didn't say anything.

"Come on, Dad," Al said under his breath.

His dad almost had the cover off, but it looked like some fasteners were preventing him from accessing the interior. Al watched the first tube dispense its liquid into the black panel box. Sweat began to form on Al's forehead and he wiped it away with the back of his wrist.

His mom mouthed the word "Here" as she took off her eyeglasses. He watched his dad give a twist to one arm of the glasses and something like a screwdriver appeared on the end. They smiled at each other. Al hadn't seen his dad or mom smile since he was seven years old. He wished he could be with them again.

His dad didn't waste any time unscrewing the panel to access the interior. As his mom moved to the side, Al's stomach sickened—he could see the whole thing was rigged with plastic C-4 explosives—enough to vaporize them if it went off.

Al jumped into bomb squad mode. His extensive training included all sorts of weapons and demolition. As a
prep school for the CIA, Junior Agents had to be ready for
anything. Turnkey was by far the best among the agents
at bomb disposal, but Alabaster was proficient enough.

Come on, Dad, cut the right wires.

His dad shook his head as the second tube dropped its
liquid into the box. Both his parents worked diligently on
the bomb, but Al could tell from their body movements
that someone was speaking to them beyond the view of
the camera.

When his dad moved to the side, Al saw several different colored wires formed into two cords from the central
container, each leading to metal sticks in the C-4. Watching
his dad work, Al's mom looked up to the ceiling and said
something. Al could see her lips move, but he didn't know
what she said. It was so frustrating to see their lips move
but not hear them. Al couldn't remember what his parents
sounded like. He had no frame of reference and didn't own
any videos of them.

The third tube funnelled its liquid into the box.

His parents consulted again and this time they contem-
plated something. His dad looked at his mom and mouthed
the word "Yes" as the fourth tube dropped its liquid into
the container. The timer was under 60 seconds to go. Al's
heart was pounding in his chest.

"Come on, get it, Dad!" Al said in the hallway aloud.
No one was around.

His dad used the snips from the other side of his mom's eyeglasses to cut through the wires connected to the C-4.

The timer didn't stop.

His dad reached out his hand to his mom and they stood there watching the bomb. Al watched the countdown...

3...

2...

1...

0...

...

...

Nothing. Nothing happened.

After a long pause, it looked like someone was talking to his parents from their body movements.

He saw his mom start talking to the ceiling again, but couldn't see her lips except for a few words as she moved her head back and forth while talking. It looked like she said '*done*' or '*game*'.

His mom turned to look at his dad and stood there staring at him for a while. Al watched his mom look up to the ceiling of the glass room and say something clear and slow while she held his dad's hand. It looked like, "We don't have the stone."

We don't have the stone?

After a moment, he watched his mom shout to the ceiling, "No!" and his dad grabbed her with a hug and whispered something to her. Al's head started to hurt and he felt hot. He wanted to feel his parents' arms around him again. His mom pulled slightly away and Al could see her say, "I love you, too." Then a massive burst of white smoke flooded into the glass room, causing their bodies to collapse to the floor.

"NO!" Al shouted.

He watched as his parents, their hands clasped, closed their eyes forever. Then the video ended.

Al collapsed to his knees in tears. He had just watched the murder of his parents.

He felt empty and alone and waves of hurt rushed through his mind. Tear drops fell and formed puddles on the wood planks where he knelt. Unaware how long he sobbed, he heard a high-pitched voice. "Alabaster Dangermond, what troubles you?" He didn't answer and he could hardly see anything around him.

The old man leaned down next to Al and did the oddest thing; at least, Al thought it was the oddest thing. The man used his long white braided beard and dabbed Al's eyes, catching the tears as they fell.

"It will be all right, Agent Dangermond. This too shall soon pass."

Because of the oddity, the pace of Al's tears lessened and soon stopped altogether. Al wiped the dripping snot from his nose with the back of his hand and turned to look at the old man next to him.

"Sensei Xu, my parents—" Al snapped his mouth shut. The warning on the email had said not to tell anyone.

"Yes?" the old Chinese man asked the teen agent.

But Al remained silent and just stared ahead, feeling a wave of exhaustion.

"It appears you must rest, Agent Dangermond. I will call for an escort to take you to your room and I will alert the Chief that you will be absent from my martial arts class today. Your mind must rest now, and we can talk tomorrow about your parents."

Chin Chin Xu radioed from his wrist bracelet for some assistance and a couple of boys came and helped Alabaster back to the dormitory room he shared with Turnkey. Al couldn't do anything but lay on his bed thinking about the email. Who sent it—the killer? Why? How could his parents have died four months after they were declared dead from an automobile accident? He lay lost in a mire of thoughts until exhaustion brought his mind to rest. He fell asleep asking, *Why did they have to die?*

4

Brothers

Alabaster Dangermond awoke to the smell of breakfast sausage.

He looked over at the clock on his bunk shelf and saw it was 6:15 in the morning. He never used an alarm—ever since he was little, he could awaken his body any time he wanted after a night of sleep. Faint streams of sunlight shone through the blinds of his small, double-person bedroom. It was a standard room at the Long Island mansion academy.

Flopping his head back onto the pillow, he cleared his mind as he stared up at the ceiling. He could hear Turnkey breathing deeply in the bunk bed below. The breakfast smells always filled their room in the morning—he guessed a duct from the kitchen must somehow wind its way into his room vent.

Al had slept in his clothes from the previous day. Someone must have helped him to bed. He pulled his wrist up to his face and turned on his watch to access his email. He clicked the video of his parents and began to watch again. He turned it off almost immediately—he felt like puking.

The Chief told me my parents died in a car wreck just after I turned seven. How could he have been wrong?

He rolled over onto his side and stared at the wall ahead, trying to clear his mind. Sunlight glinted off the objects hanging on the wall. Those in the U.S.A. kept few personal items, but Al still had medals hanging on the wall from years ago. He began winning rock-climbing competitions at an early age and on his seventh birthday, he became the youngest junior youth climbing champion in the country.

Accomplishment was not the real reason he kept them on the wall, though.

It was a week after he turned seven when he was told of the tragic car wreck that had killed his parents. After that, his interest in sports competition ended. The medals were one of his only reminders of them.

Turnkey stirred and awoke. "Al? You up there, man?"

"Yeah, I'm here."

"Yo. What happened to you? You never showed for tennis with me and Mary-Anne, and then I found you sleeping here in the room. You all right, man?"

Al was *not* all right. He had seen his parents murdered. The email said not to tell anyone, but Al didn't want to lie to his best friend.

"Things are not cool, Turnkey. I got an email yesterday and it reminded me of my parents." Turnkey got out of his bed and stood up next to the bunk. "What did it say?"

Al had thought his friend wouldn't inquire further, but now he had to spill the beans.

"Well, for starters it said that if I told you what it said, the person would kill me and my friends."

Turnkey scrunched his forehead. "Whoa. Wait. I thought this was about your parents?"

Alabaster thought it would just be easier to let Turnkey have his watch. He turned in his bed to face the wall, while Turnkey sat in a chair at his desk and watched the video.

After a while, Turnkey paused it. "How did your parents know how to stop a bomb?"

Al remained quiet and Turnkey continued to watch the video to its end.

"Man, I'm sorry, Al, but yo, maybe this is fake. I thought you said your parents died in a car wreck."

"That's what the Chief told me after I won nationals. He said they died in a car wreck in London." Al shifted back to his other side to face Turnkey and then sat up on the bed with his feet dangling over the edge.

"Yo, man, we've gotta show the Chief. We have to clear this up. Maybe this video footage is before the car wreck happened?"

"No. No way. We can't show the Chief. If ZM knows who I am and knows about the secret U.S.A., we can't risk telling the Chief or anyone else. It's a risk just showing you. Maybe ZM is a mole in the U.S.A.—how else could they know about us?

"Yo, no way, homie. Nobody connected to us is in on this. This is evidence of your parents' involvement in something serious. It's dated seven years ago. Everything is linked to this ZM person." Both teens paused.

Turnkey raised his eyebrows. "Who were your parents?"

Al thought he knew, but time had faded his memory. He loved and missed them deeply. Once sharp, the last seven years had dulled even the most memorable of details—the song they always sang to him at bedtime, the rough skin of his father's hand when he held it, even the smell of his mom's lasagna and the apron she always wore —it was so hard to remember the details. They were a faded distant love, leaving a hole in his heart.

He looked over at the picture of them on his desk. It was the day he became the junior climbing champion— May 24th, his seventh birthday. His parents made visits on weekends to the sports academy, but his training was year round, so he never went back to his house in Newport, Rhode Island.

Al sighed. "It's so hard to remember who my parents were. We lived in a brown house, but it wasn't anything special."

Turnkey handed back the watch and Al turned it off. "You think they were agents? I mean, they tried to disable that bomb. Weren't they in construction?"

"No, they were engineers. They could easily disable a machine like that. I guess them being agents only crossed my mind a couple of times since I ended up with the Chief as my guardian. But really I think that is just because I was orphaned while doing the sports competition under the Universal Sports Academy banner. I think my parents must have thought of the Chief as the best role model for me, if they died."

Turnkey frowned. "Homie, we have to tell the Chief."

"No, TK. We have to keep this quiet. Until I can figure out what is going on, we can't tell anyone."

"Yo, dawg, you mean *we*, right? Until *we* figure this out. I'm gonna help, man. That's what brothers do for each other."

Al looked at his friend. The Chief had paired them together when they were twelve years old, after three years of initial training. Now each fourteen, Al could not imagine a better best friend.

"Thanks, Turnkey."

Turnkey stood up and clapped his hands together. "Yo, man. Get changed and let's go get some breakfast. That smell of sausage always makes me so hungry."

5

Prepping for the CIA

Al spent all his waking time thinking about his parents. Unfortunately, he hardly had any time to talk to Turnkey about the details because Mr. Underwood made him a slave from early morning to late at night when he wasn't in class.

He cleaned just about every room in the mansion, sometimes before and after the room was used. Al had a checklist for each room and what was needed—chairs in their place. *Check*. Trash taken out. *Check*. Markers for whiteboards all accounted for. *Check*. So many details to cover per room. He didn't sluff off at any time knowing the Chief was watching him on the tracking chip in his shoulder. Al had no idea how much work Mr. Underwood and his staff had to perform to run the house so efficiently for the agents. This punishment pretty much stunk.

Al had prepared some of the rooms for the CIA agents who were staying at the mansion to oversee the Agent Trials. The place was abuzz and all the talk was about the Agent Trials. Both Junior Agents and the Trainees, the nine to twelve-years-olds, scampered about with the hopes of meeting some of the CIA agents. Trainees did most of their agent education in simulators and a few of the brightest had the opportunity to work at analyst computer stations on real CIA cases as part of their training.

The night before the Trials, Turnkey and Al finally had a chance to talk in their bedroom. Turnkey was in the middle of a set of sit-ups when Al turned from his desk and looked at him. "So I've been thinking more about my parents."

"Come up with anything?" Turnkey continued crunching the abdominal workout.

Al ran his hand through his hair. "I think maybe they must have been kidnapped. I mean, I know they left me a lot of money in my trust and I don't have any sisters or brothers—"

"Yo, dawg, whatcha call me?"

"You know what I mean, *brother.*" Al laughed. "So maybe their kidnapper faked their car death because he wanted money. I think my mom was talking about a stone in the video. Maybe they owned diamonds or something and the kidnapper wanted that?"

Turnkey finished his sit-ups and looked at Al. "Yo, I thought she said *stone* too. Did they leave you diamonds?"

Al shook his head. "No. They just left me money in a trust. The Chief gives me a monthly amount from it as my guardian, but he hasn't ever said anything much about it."

Turnkey stood up and wiped his forehead with the back of his hand. "You still think we should keep this video from the Chief?"

Al threw Turnkey a small towel. "Yeah. We just need time to figure it out."

Turnkey wiped down his head with the towel and looked at Al. "We could bring Mary-Anne in on this to help us. She could run a sneaky trace on that email and find where it came from."

"I thought about her too, but I want to try between us first," Al said.

Turnkey yawned. "Well, when we both pass the Agent Trials tomorrow and head to Langley, we might be able to use CIA resources to find out more. But yo, we gotta turn in early for tomorrow—it's gonna be intense."

Al agreed and said goodnight and the guys got into their bunks. The Agent Trials had been the least of his concerns over the last few days, but tomorrow he would give it his sole attention. Failing the Agent Trials meant expulsion from the Undercover Secret Agency and the end of everything he wanted.

~

The next morning, the Junior Agents waited outside the mansion for a company bus to take them from Long Island to New York City. Al was anxious all night and hardly slept because he couldn't stop thinking about the Agent Trials. He downed an energy drink. It boosted him enough that he jogged in place to release some energy as he waited. As he ran in place, he tried to concentrate on different scenarios from his classes that he might encounter in the Trials.

The Undercover Secret Agency prep-school had a strong record of recruiting the best students and many of the top agents at the CIA initially came from the Universal Sports Academy. For the few that could handle it, they would go into the CIA Black-Ops section and become Field Agents, if they did well in the Agent Trials. He felt like he'd already run a marathon by the time the bus arrived.

Turnkey tapped on Al's shoulder when they got on the bus. "Yo, can I have the window seat?"

"Sure, TK." Al let his partner pass and they both sat down together.

As the bus began to pull away from the main circle drive, they looked out and saw Mary-Anne wave good-bye from one of the mansion windows. The guys smiled and waved back. When the bus pulled onto the main street, each put on their headphones to listen to music.

As the rural landscapes became urban outside the window, Al continued to think about the tests. Everyone knew the Chief kept the past Trials secret and agents were forbidden to discuss them once they participated. How would the CIA change them this year? Al began to feel a pit forming in his stomach. Had his courses prepared him enough? Alongside the classes taught by tutors in normal school subjects, he had taken special classes for CIA preparation. Weapons & demolition, martial arts, secret codes & cryptology, intelligence gathering & observation, and HSV—High-Speed-Vehicle training—were among some of the classes. He had done well, but nobody could compare to Turnkey or Mary-Anne. Turnkey was the top Junior Agent and Mary-Anne had always been ahead of everyone, even though she was only thirteen.

Left behind at the mansion, she would have passed the Trials if given the chance. She excelled at everything, but especially computers and technology. Everyone called her a genius because she had become a Junior Agent when she was only ten years old. Her brilliance in engineering allowed her to have her own laboratory as a lead scientist on Blue Level at the downtown U.S.A. Headquarters in the city, where she often worked creating helpful gadgets. Nobody could compare to Mary-Anne, but as Al looked around the bus, he felt like everyone was a better agent than him. He felt sick to his stomach and he started to pick at his fingernails. He had given all his thought to the email and video over the last few days, instead of concentrating on the Trials when the Chief announced them.

The company bus arrived at the downtown Universal Sports Academy building and parked on the street since it was too tall to go into the underground parking garage. Alabaster and Turnkey followed the other Junior Agents as they stepped out of the bus and entered a side door into the skyscraper. The U.S.A. headquarters was hidden below the main building of the Universal Sports Academy. The deep secret location had softer rock than at the mansion, making it an ideal place to dig decades ago.

The Junior Agents were led to a prep room on the first level of the building. The room was large and had cushioned chairs with a couple of windows that looked out into the hall. A flat-panel television was on the wall, with everyone's name displayed. Two men and a woman wearing black suits were waiting for them. The dark-haired woman told everyone to take a seat.

The woman explained that the Agent Trials would be taken individually and that tests would take about an hour to complete. All the Junior Agents looked at each other in surprise—Al thought it would take the whole day, and apparently so did everyone else.

The woman raised her voice and said they would only do skills examinations and it was going to happen in the same place the Chief normally set up his Trials on Indigo Level—below in the secret HQ. After it was over, each Junior Agent was supposed to meet with a CIA Agent to discuss their results.

Al sat forward in his chair and started to bounce one of his legs. He was skillful, but his best work came from climbing tests and paper examinations. This Trial was not in his favor. Al looked over at Turnkey, who showed no sign of being nervous. The woman explained they would not go to the weapons hall but enter the *Field Agent Inquiry Location* door. He had passed that door on Indigo several times when heading to advanced weapons training to learn how to shoot guns and rockets. Al always wondered what was behind that door.

The Junior Agents were told they would go in alphabetical order, according to their last name. That put Al in fourth position. The flat-panel on the wall indicated when a tested agent was finished. Al looked over at Turnkey, who was immersed in music with headphones on. Al closed his eyes and tried to think about all the exams they might throw at him. When he thought of bomb-defusing training, he couldn't shake thoughts about his parents. A flood of sadness rushed through his body and he felt hot. Why were they killed? What was the stone? Al pictured his mom and dad and missed them...

"Alabaster Dangermond. You're up now," the woman said, tapping him on the shoulder. He opened his eyes and looked and saw his name was on the flat-panel—he must have fallen asleep.

Turnkey pulled off his headphones. "Go get it, Al. You'll be great, yo."

Al rubbed his eyes and turned to his friend. "Thanks, bro." He gave Turnkey a double-bump with his fist and left the room.

The thirty-nine story Headquarters building had 28 high-speed elevators, but members of the secret U.S.A. only used one specific elevator to go down, number 12. Pressing the elevator button, the doors opened. Al stepped in and the doors closed.

"I.D. card please," said a female voice in the closed elevator. Alabaster usually thought the HQ elevator voice sounded soothing but he hardly noticed her this time—he was trying to think about what the first test would be. He rolled his shoulders to try and loosen them up as he pulled out his ID.

Al swiped his card through the card reader and the elevator lights turned red. Several laser beams scanned the elevator.

"Full security scan complete. Welcome back, Agent Dangermond," said the elevator voice. "You are instructed to proceed to the Field Agent Inquiry Location on level Indigo."

The elevator began its 700-foot rapid descent.

He had reached the Agent Trials.

6

The Agent Trials

The elevator stopped. "Welcome to Indigo Level. Please watch your step."

Seeing the familiar purple color on the walls, Al stepped out of the elevator and walked down the hall. Junior Agents came here to learn weapons training and they always passed the same door on their way to the weapons hall. This time, Al was going to see what was behind the door he'd passed hundreds of times before.

Al stopped and peered at the metal door, etched with white letters that read *Field Agent Inquiry Location – AGENT TRIALS ONLY*. Almost all the doors at Headquarters were made of thick glass, but this door was solid metal and Al had never seen anyone enter it.

It wasn't the first time he'd noticed the capital letters

engraved on the door spelled *FAIL*. Al shook out his arms and stretched to loosen up. He blew out a long breath as he reached out to open the door.

The door opened inward and he saw darkness ahead of him. It was hot and smelled musty and damp, a lot like Turnkey's socks after playing basketball. He stepped across the threshold and walked forward into a dimly lit hall. The dark hallway floor had small puddles of water everywhere. The door slammed shut, startling him.

"Run!" was the only word he heard echoing its way down the hall as a smoky gas started filling the passage.

Without thinking, Al took off sprinting down the hall as fast as he could, splashing through puddles. The heat in the hall was making him sweat profusely. Flashes of red appeared behind him—laser beams were systematically shooting down from the ceiling.

Looking back, he could see them penetrating through the smoky fog. They were coming from behind him as he ran, but he was fast enough to outpace them—until his body slammed hard into the black concrete wall and he lay dazed from the impact.

The beams were coming.

He rubbed his eyes and looked back down the hall—the laser beams were shooting down from the ceiling about 20 feet from him. Al shook his head back and forth to clear the daze. He randomly pushed on the walls around him as fast as he could but nothing gave way. It was a dead end. His chest felt tight and his throat was dry. He wished he had spent his last few days thinking through possible scenarios for the Trials instead of obsessing over the email about his parents.

Al blew out a breath and looked quickly at his surroundings. He had nothing with him to block the beams so he looked for a secret switch on the wall. Quickly searching, Al saw a rectangle etched into the wall near the bottom and he pressed it.

The lower portion of the wall opened up with white light beyond as smoke poured into the new opening. Al dove into the hole. The lasers hit the spot where he had just stood, missing him by inches.

Coughing from the musty stench, Al stood up. He put his hand on his chest and felt his heart beating hard. A noise behind him drew his attention—the wall had closed back up, sealing the laser hallway from his view. He looked around at his new environment.

The new room had two parts—he stood on one side and in front of him was a glass wall that he could see through. It was dark on the other side.

Thankfully, the Trial taskmasters weren't completely heartless and left a water bottle on a table. Al guzzled the whole thing quickly, without giving thought to whether it was part of the test. The water tasted weird, like plastic.

He put the empty bottle on the table and waited. Becoming restless, Al began to pace in the room and investigated the glass wall, but he found nothing. Then he heard a woman's voice speaking from what sounded like an intercom.

"Al? Alabaster, is that you?" As if in a dream, a life-like image of a woman appeared in front of him on the other side of the glass wall. She was dressed in the same blue shirt she wore in the picture from his bedroom. Her light brown hair flowed in a ghostly form, like a hologram.

"*Mom?*"

7

The Real Trial

Al pressed his face and hands against the glass divider. He knew she couldn't be real, but the ache pounded hard in his chest. His breath fogged up the glass as he looked at her. She didn't say anything more, but hers was the voice he remembered. It was what his heart longed for most.

Then his mom vanished. It was as if the past gave him back life, only to snatch it from his soul. He yelled out, "Hey!"

"Please solve this riddle, Agent Dangermond," said a voice. "You find a rotten carrot, a few small stones, and a pipe lying together in the middle of a field. What happened at that location?"

"Wait? What?" He had missed the whole list. He closed his eyes to try and remember, but he couldn't do it—all he could think of was his mom. He sighed loudly as he raked his finger through his hair and could feel the sweat coming off his palms. Things were moving way too fast.

Al scratched the top of his head and slumped his shoulders. "I don't know. Can you please repeat the list?"

After what seemed like an eternity, the voice repeated the riddle, "You find a rotten carrot, a few small stones, and a pipe lying together in the middle of a field. What happened at that location?" This time Alabaster didn't miss anything.

"Someone made a snowman with a carrot as a nose, eyes with the stones, and the pipe in his mouth, and after, the snowman melted."

Al heard a click and a door to his right opened. "Proceed," the voice said.

He furrowed his brow and looked back at the dark side behind the glass, where his mother had appeared. He felt sick and mad at himself. Even with years of training, his lack of preparation and focus during the past few days was showing. He could hear his mom's voice in his head, the voice he had forgotten, saying his name over and over as he turned and walked through the open door.

Al walked into a small room that had a wooden chair next to a table. On top were two items: a bottle of water and a map. He took a sip and stood next to the table investigating the map.

"Sit," the voice commanded.

Taking a seat, he continued to look at the map. It was a regional map of an obscure place in Europe, the country of Albania. He saw something scribbled on the map in pencil, but he couldn't make it out. As he examined the map, the lights went out in the room until it was pitch black like a cave.

After a span, the lights came back on. Alabaster shook his head and rubbed his eyes—the entire room had been rearranged. Decorations of seaside scenes with labels like Florida, California, and Vancouver adorned all four walls and on one part there was an odd scene of Durres, a seaside town in Albania. The lights went out again.

Expecting the change, he listened intently, but heard nothing beyond the noise he made in his chair. The lights beamed on again. Instead of decorations, there appeared four different movies, each on one of the four walls. The movies were black and white and they showed various scenes. Al looked around and took in as much as possible. He sought references to Albania. *There.* On one wall, he saw the double-eagle flag of Albania. The lights went out again.

When the lights came back on, he only heard a voice ask, "How many references did you see, Agent Dangermond?"

Al looked up at the ceiling. "How many references to what?"

The voice repeated the same question. Al didn't like this game. Was he supposed to guess how many references to Albania had he observed?

"Look, I'll give you a number if you tell me how many of what?" he said back.

After a long pause, "How many references to each place did you see?"

Al had done this before in class, but it had been so long since he practiced. He felt sick again and heard water slosh around in his stomach as he moved in his chair. *I can't let my emotions get the better of me.*

Closing his eyes, he thought through his time in the room. Trying to process what he could remember, he determined there were four locations.

"I saw Albania, Florida, Vancouver, and California. There were four references to Albania and three references to the others."

"Incorrect, Agent Dangermond. There were six references to each of those locations," the voice said.

Six? "Come on," Al said to himself, pounding his fist on the table.

A hidden door opened in the wall.

"Go now," the voice said.

Al stood up and hit his hand on his thigh. He walked through the door into a new dark room and the door shut behind him. As he looked, the room brightened. It was all white with a small end table that had tools next to a large door. The door had what looked like an electronic lock. On the wall was a flat-panel screen.

"Open the door as fast as you can," the voice commanded. "You are being timed."

A stopwatch began counting on the flat-panel screen. Al took the flat-head screwdriver and noticed his palm was sweaty. With the tool, he began prying off the lock panel. It popped off in seconds. Underneath he found a standard electronic lock.

Yes. He had studied the design and practiced on this type in training. He worked more quickly and grabbed the tool snips to cut the white and green wires to bypass the lock circuit. As he moved the snips in place, Al noticed something different—a short black wire.

That's not right.

He paused to take a closer look. The short wire was bypassing both the white and the green wires, making them useless—if he cut them, the lock would still function. He noticed the green wire tucked into a different port. If he cut the green, it would fry the lock mechanism with an electric burst and fuse it—it would never open.

"Whoa," Al said under his breath. He looked up at the timer; two minutes had passed.

He double-checked the locking mechanism and saw the red wire was the only one that would bypass the circuit and open the door. All his training taught him never to cut the red wire. Turnkey had hammered it into him.

Turnkey is always better at electronics.

His gut told him not to cut it because red always meant failure. He looked one more time for anything out of place, but saw nothing. He had to cut the red wire. All logical reason said he had to cut it. Taking the snips, he sliced the red wire.

Al immediately heard the door click and it opened!

The timer stopped at 4:24.

Al jumped up in the air with a fist pump, "Yes!"

He stepped toward the door. "Am I done here?"

"Yes, Agent Dangermond. Proceed to the next room."

He walked down a short tunnel into an area that looked like an underground subway station. There was a one-person vehicle on the track that went into a tunnel.

"Get in," the voice commanded.

Al stepped in and buckled himself. There were no controls and the vehicle started moving forward quickly on the rails, zipping past lights in the tunnel and descending. He emerged from the tunnel into a place that looked like the real world, but was a manufactured landscape in a gigantic underground room. Before him was a skyscraper construction site, with a tall building made of some completed floors and exposed girders. The metal girders formed the frame of a skyscraper. Al got out of the vehicle and heard a shout.

Looking up, he saw the source—a construction worker was dangling from a girder.

"Help! Someone, help!" the worker shouted.

Al dashed to the construction lift. He hit the control and the makeshift elevator took him up to the most recently completed level—floor number 5, fifty feet off the ground. Three more levels up, the man dangled on a girder that hung over the street, about eight stories down.

Al yelled up to the man. "Hang on! I'm coming." Their eyes connected and Al could see the terror on his face. There was no clear path up the girders but Al used his rock-climbing knowledge to form his plan.

The man slipped further down on his broken harness and screamed again.

"Help! Please, help me!"

Al bolted forward to the nearest girder and shimmied up fast. He walked across a girder toward the man, keeping his hands out to his side to balance himself.

"Hang on, I'm almost there!" Alabaster's palms were

sweaty and slick. He wished he had some climbing chalk to keep them dry.

At the next horizontal beam, he made his way toward the man.

"Please, I can't hold on! My harness is broken and I'm going to fall!" the man shouted.

Al saw a coiled rope on the girder in front of him and grabbed it. He moved toward the safety harness latch that held the man in mid-air.

"Help, please!" he said as the harness ripped further. Al strained to reach the man, but he was just out of reach. Al secured the coiled rope to a girder support and tied himself up.

"Hang on! I'm going to grab onto you!" Al braced himself and then jumped at the man just below him.

Upon impact, the man's harness ripped apart. The construction worker grabbed onto Al as they fell.

In freefall, the rope came to its end quicker than Al expected. The hard jerk jolted both parties and the man lost his grip. Al's palms were too sweaty to keep his grasp on the man and he watched in horror as the worker plummeted toward death, far below.

In a blur, a large rectangular object emerged, rising up from the ground. The man hit the ground and Al saw waves of air across fabric. *A cushion.*

Al realized he was in the simulation—the Agent Trials— and this was part of his test. That made his side hurt even more from the jerk of the rope as he hung there dangling above the simulation. The man was real, but the danger had not been.

"Prepare to fall, Agent Dangermond," said the familiar test voice. A laser cut through his rope and he fell on the cushion. The construction actor gave him a hand and let him know the Trials were over. He pointed to an exit door and Alabaster walked down a very long, lonely hallway to a small elevator that took him up to meet a CIA agent for his debrief. Al knew he had failed some parts of the test—but had he passed enough to become an Assistant Agent?

8

Failed Hopes

"Alabaster?" bellowed the Chief, hearing a knock on the door.

His assistant peeked his head into the room, "No, sir, not yet. But I just received confirmation from debrief on Green Level that he has been diverted to your office for his debriefing."

The large man moved away from the windows that looked out on Madison Avenue near Grand Central Station in New York City.

"Adequate." He thumped his way out of the double doors into the foyer. Perkins backed away, giving the large man plenty of room to maneuver.

The man looked at Perkins' immaculately clean desk and then looked at the assistant, who was holding a clipboard. "I wonder if he's already figured it out himself—he's a bright young man."

"Uh…Yes, sir…Maybe, sir?"

"Perkins! I was just thinking aloud. I don't need an answer."

Perkins looked down at his clipboard. "Uh…right, sir. Yes, sir." Perkins muttered under his breath as he rolled his eyes, hoping his boss did not see it.

The large man turned back toward his double-doors. "Well…When he gets here, send him right in." He went back into his office.

"Uh….Okay…sir…," Perkins said as the doors slammed shut.

~

Al sat down in one of the chairs in the Chief's office. It was his second visit here and Al felt an overwhelming sadness. His heart began to sink when the agent on Green level told him to come here to debrief, but now it was worse. The last time he was in this office, the Chief had shared about the death of his parents. Maybe it was better to hear the bad news about failing from his guardian than from some senior agent. The large boss was sitting behind an enormous desk, looking right at him.

"Alabaster, I am going to get straight to the point—you failed the Trials," the man said. "You were tested on five essential skills for Assistant Agent status: physical speed, mental toughness, technological expertise, observation, and courage. You only passed three of the five. You lost all concentration with the simple trick of your mother and you allowed yourself to be distracted by the Albanian map.

What do you have to say for yourself?" The stern look of the Chief said it all.

His career as a secret agent was over. Al looked away toward the windows as the pit in his stomach grew. He ran one of his hands through his hair and breathed deeply.

The teen agent looked back at the big man and answered him. "I don't have a good excuse, Chief. Maybe I let my emotions cloud my judgment. Probably—"

"Probably nothing, Alabaster. If you don't pay attention to the details, you're going to get yourself killed as a field agent. And you've always worn your heart on your sleeve. It's an asset and a curse. It gives you great passion and courage, but it is your greatest weakness too. You can't let your emotions come to the surface or you'll be deceived by the enemy. I know you miss your parents, but you can't let your love for them be used against you. You have to guard your emotions. You have to guard your heart."

"But, sir, my parents," Al said, looking at the Chief's stern face. He remembered the warning from the email and quickly withdrew his next remark. "Yes, sir." Al's shoulders slumped.

"As it stands, you're not accepted at Langley and it's my call if I want to keep you on until you're sixteen. But I have a better reason why I'm not sending you packing," the Chief said as he stood from his chair and looked out at the Manhattan skyline. "Your parents."

"My parents, sir?"

"Yes, Alabaster. You see, my boy, your parents were agents under my supervision before the Undercover Secret

Agency began. They worked for me doing covert and clandestine missions when I was with the CIA."

Turnkey was right. The Chief was more to my parents. "But my parents were engineers; they designed electrical equipment, right?"

"Yes. Your parents were electrical engineers. But, they used that as their cover. They spent years with the CIA, fighting international criminals.

Al sat thinking until the Chief spoke. "Alabaster, I know this must come as a shock to you."

"Not really, Chief. I mean, I've been actually wondering about it lately. I thought it was because you were the head supervisor while I was at the sports academy and it was natural you would be my guardian if they died. But I guess if they were part of the CIA, then that explains how I ended up here. I've always wondered, but it makes sense."

The Chief nodded.

Al scratched his head and swallowed hard. "You said they died in a car wreck. Was it a mission?"

The Chief turned to look at the skyline out the window.

"Yes. You were seven years old. I sent them on a mission to Scotland to infiltrate a crime network operating in a remote chain of isles. They flew into London and on their way north, their car was attacked. If you remember, I came to you and told you they died in a car wreck. That was true. What I didn't tell you was their car caught fire and exploded in northern London and they died. It was so powerful and hot, nothing was left. We suspected a crime network but the trail went cold in the search for the killer.

The case was never solved, but I'm convinced it was not a simple accident. I am very sorry for your loss, Alabaster."

So their death in the car wreck was a cover-up.

Al looked up at the large man. "Well, what did you do to recover them?"

The Chief furled his forehead and raised an eyebrow. "Recover them? Their bodies were incinerated." The large man gave Al a quizzical look. Al shouldn't have asked that. The Chief didn't know his parents were alive after the car wreck.

Alabaster tried to recover quickly, "So if the case was never solved, then is it still open? Can I see the file of the investigation?"

The Chief frowned. "The case is closed as never solved. I don't think it's a good idea for you to see the file."

Al thought he shouldn't press his luck. "What do my parents have to do with my failure in the Agent Trials?"

The Chief moved his large body over to the desk and sat down in his leather chair. "You failed the CIA Trials, but you didn't fail mine. This may be a CIA prep-school, but I am still in charge of the Undercover Secret Agency. I have an agreement with the CIA, but that doesn't mean they can dictate who comes or who goes. You failed *them*, but you didn't fail *me*—you would have passed my designed Trials. Plus, I owe it to your parents to keep training you. Normally, you wouldn't even have a shot at Langley until you were sixteen anyway. I'm keeping you around because it's my call."

Maybe I should let him see the video.

Al felt grateful for another chance, but the look on the Chief's face and his reluctance to share the file on his parents made Al feel uneasy. He decided to continue hiding the email from the Chief. "So what now? Am I going back to the mansion?"

The look on the Chief's face was not a happy one. "Yes, you will be going back. But you are going back alone. The CIA is taking all of my other Junior Agents to Langley." The large man clenched his right hand into a fist and looked away from Al. "They are heading south tonight. Their things will be shipped to them from the mansion."

Al stood up. "What? Turnkey is going to Langley? You're splitting us up?"

The Chief looked at Alabaster. "Sit down, Agent!"

Al sat as the large man stood up with his huge belly partially resting on the edge of his desk. "This is not my doing. Yes. Agent Keystone has been promoted. It is likely you will not see him for some time. The new Assistant Agents will be going to the CIA Farm at Camp Peary down in Williamsburg, Virginia, for two years of covert training before they assume their normal analyst duties at Langley. When agents go to the Farm, all communication with the outside world is restricted—only hand-written letters to parents are permitted. Every graduate of the Farm assumes a new covert set of identities. I'm sorry, Alabaster, but you won't see Turnkey or any of your other classmates again for at least two years, maybe more."

"More?"

The big man shifted his weight and his belly moved

off the desk. "I expect you to be promoted when you turn sixteen, and it's likely with this new protocol that you will head to the Farm at least for a while when your classmates go to Langley. If that happens, you will possibly have a couple of years of communication restrictions too."

"That's four years, Chief!"

The man pounded his fist down on his desk. "Yes, Agent Dangermond! Calm yourself!"

I'm not going to see Turnkey for four years? Al felt hot and like he wanted to throw up. His best friend had just been ripped from his life.

9

Agent Keystone

The CIA senior agent stood up and shook Turnkey's hand before the teenager could even sit down in the debrief room on Green Level. "Congratulations, Agent Keystone. You've passed every Agent Trial test with perfect marks. I am promoting you to Assistant Agent status, effective immediately. I've never said this to anyone, but you show signs of becoming a superior agent. Your record is spotless and no one has ever passed with a perfect score before, according to the data the Chief provided the CIA. You did it."

Turnkey sat down and felt tingling goosebumps on his skin. It was like he had just swished a 3-point buzzer beater on the basketball court—nothing-but-net for the championship.

The words from the CIA agent, "*You did it*," reminded him of his mom. She had said the same thing when he became a Junior Agent. As a single mom, she had sacrificed to get him into the Universal Sports Academy to work with the best athletes. Now, as part of the U.S.A., he had the chance to make a real difference in the world fighting criminals. It was everything he had worked for.

The CIA agent smiled at him. "Agent Keystone, you excelled in each exercise, but your observation skills impressed me most. You provided the exact number of references for Vancouver, Albania, California, and Florida. Therefore, I am recommending you for accelerated SSO— oh, sorry…I mean the Specialized Skills Officer training, to enter the National Clandestine Service in the CIA. You officially cannot become a CIA Secret Agent until you are eighteen, but the officer-training program will give you more skills than you would receive at the Farm at Camp Peary. You will be part of an elite group and it automatically qualifies you to be on the short-list for promotion one day to CIA Director."

Turnkey raised his eyebrows. "I could become the Director of the CIA?"

"Yes, anyone who has gone through the SSO training is automatically considered for the job, but you will have to wait until you are thirty for that promotion. I cannot confirm or deny the association with past Directors, but I can assure you if you do the SSO training, it is the quick path to leadership. Without SSO, it's unlikely to happen."

"Yo."

The agent shuffled through some papers on the desk. "As you know, since you've passed, we will transport you this evening. You will travel by plane with the other new Assistant Agents down to Camp Peary to begin your training. We will send for your things at the mansion."

Al. How did Al do?

Turnkey smiled at the man. "Sir, do you know how the other Junior Agents did?"

The senior agent jotted a note down on paper and then answered. "No, I don't. I'm only assigned to you. But you can find out at the dinner before we fly out. Is there anything else?"

Turnkey shook his head. "No, sir."

The man stood and held out his hand, "Welcome to the CIA, Agent Keystone."

∼

Turnkey grabbed the food and put it on his tray. All the Junior Agents were in the Universal Sports Academy skyscraper cafeteria, except Al. Turnkey sat down alone at a table for four. He acknowledged his classmates around him with a sharp head bob.

What happened to Al?

He picked up his bread roll and started eating. It didn't take long to devour everything on his plate.

Al must have gotten hurt or something. He couldn't have failed.

Turnkey finished off his second glass of milk and slumped in his chair. As he looked forward, he saw Alabaster Dangermond rush through the opening to the cafeteria.

"Al!"

Alabaster ran over to Turnkey and gave him a slap hug as they clasped one hand.

Turnkey looked at Al. "Yo! What's up, homie? Are you all right?"

Al looked around at everyone staring at him. Turnkey saw he was pale. They sat down and Al spoke quietly, "I failed, Turnkey. I failed the Agent Trials. But the Chief is keeping me on at the Agency, at least until I'm sixteen. He told me you passed and his assistant Perkins told me all of you were down here eating. So I came down to see you to say goodbye."

Al explained in detail what the Chief had told him.

Turnkey smiled. "That's everything, dawg. Except, why was there a cover-up?"

Al didn't know what to say.

Turnkey told Alabaster about his promotion to the SSO training and that he might have a shot at becoming the CIA Director one day.

"Bro! That's sport'n, TK—you as Director of the CIA. Man."

"Yo, but that's not cool if we aren't together. Four years apart—you're my brother, man."

Al gave a deep sigh. "There's nothing we can do about it. I'm just gonna have to pursue my parents' murder without you, if we can't talk for four years."

Turnkey shook his head. "Not cool, homie. You're my best friend. Man, we've been partners for two years." Turnkey took a drink of water. "We can't let this happen, Al."

Al shrugged his shoulders. "But, there's nothing we can do, TK."

Turnkey stood up. "Yes. There is."

~

"No, you can't go in there. The Chief is in a meeting with the CIA," Perkins said, standing up behind his desk as the teenagers came into the foyer.

Turnkey was too fast for him. He opened the door to the Chief's skyscraper office and walked in.

"Hey!" Perkins yelled as Alabaster closed the Chief's door, shutting the assistant out.

The Chief stood up. "What is the meaning of this intrusion? You two, get out of here!"

Turnkey's CIA evaluator in the Trials was sitting comfortably in a chair in front of the large desk of the boss and turned to look at the two teenagers.

Perkins opened the door and looked in.

"You can't fail Al, Chief," Turnkey said. "He's gotta go to the Farm."

The Chief frowned. "Look, Agent Keystone. I've heard of your promotion directly from your evaluator, but that gives you no right to barge into my office and demand anything. Alabaster is staying put at the mansion and he will resume normal training duties there."

The room went silent.

Turnkey looked at Al and then turned toward the Chief. "Then I request to be reassigned to the mansion. I am turning down the promotion to the SSO training."

"What?" yelled the Chief. The man turned red. Al thought he actually saw steam come off his head. "Now you listen here, Agent Keystone. You will go to the SSO training and you will perform with excellence like you have under me."

Turnkey stood taller. "Sir. With all due respect, I am turning down the promotion. I believe having Agent Dangermond as my partner outweighs the promotion."

He turned to look at the CIA evaluator sitting in the chair. "Thank you for the promotion, sir. At this time, I will have to decline the offer and stay at the Undercover Secret Agency until I'm sixteen."

"Turnkey!" the Chief yelled.

The CIA evaluator stood up. "Well, son, if you feel that way then perhaps you aren't ready for the SSO training like I thought. I'm sure you don't understand what you are giving up, but if you are not willing to put forth the effort, then I'm not going to promote you. Consider the offer withdrawn."

The CIA man reached out his hand and Turnkey shook it. Then he turned to the big man, "Chief," and gave a nod before walking out of the room.

Turnkey and Al stood in front of the Chief in silence. The man was even redder than before. He pointed his thick finger to the door and yelled, "Get out!"

The two agents scurried out of the office as fast as possible. As they ran past Perkins, Al looked at his best friend, who had just given up the Farm, the SSO, and the fast-track to becoming the Director of the CIA.

10

Moonshadow Syndicate

Eleven criminals entered the dark room, each from their own door. Many of them looked across the long table at one another and gave a slight nod. None smiled.

Per previous instruction, the eleven stood silently behind their own leather chairs, as was the tradition established by their leader, Moonshae. As they waited, some looked down at the dark mahogany boardroom table with its crescent moon etched in the center.

The crescent shape was lightly colored next to a dark part of the moon. It was the dark part, the moon shadow, which was most important for this group. They took their name, the Moonshadow Syndicate, from their leader.

"Where is he?" One of the men, wearing a pinstriped suit, drummed his fingers vigorously on the top of his chair.

"Shut up, Darcy. You know we're supposed to remain silent," said a short man across the table.

Darcy smiled. "Rubbish to that, mate. I, for one, am sick of Moonshae's little games. He used to own me, but I found where he held my daughter captive. She's safe now and so are all the rest of my family. He's not going to blackmail me anymore."

Darcy looked around the room and tapped his heart. "Mates, today I suggest we elect a new leader." He flashed an epoxy pistol from inside his suit coat. The hard plastic gun would have been easily overlooked by Moonshae's extensive security system. Every time the eleven gathered, they passed through a metal detector and left all weapons behind before they entered the boardroom. This time, Darcy had gotten his deadly weapon through unnoticed.

A woman with scarlet hair shook her head. "You're pretty stupid if you think he will be tricked, Darcy," she said. Others chuckled.

A large man wearing a dark blazer spoke up, "I will support new leadership." Some looked surprised but nodded at Kwame, the man from South Africa.

As the group continued the debate, Moonshae laughed as he watched them from his flat-panel screen in the adjacent room.

"When will they learn?" he said to the thief. "They have no respect for tradition. Don't they understand what I am trying to do?" The thief, masked in black from head to toe, remained silent.

The boss flipped off the screen and stood up. He looked

down and straightened his white suit and adjusted his tie. Putting his fingers together, he cracked his knuckles. "Time for a lesson." He picked up his cane and looked at it.

The cane was old and ornate and he took care as he unscrewed the pommel and pressed a button on the stick. "Open the door," he commanded the thief.

The door opened and Dr. Zerick Moonshae stepped into the dark boardroom, followed by the thief, who took a position near the wall behind him. The eleven quickly ceased their debate and the room fell completely silent. Moonshae approached the table and sat down; the others followed his lead.

"Friends. Before I give the floor to each of you for your reports, I would like to tell you I have finally made a breakthrough. My thief has acquired one of the stones I've been seeking, thanks to Kwame's willingness to provide the architectural plans for the Union Buildings in Pretoria." Zerick then looked over at a man named Heeto. The Japanese crime lord, Tosaka Heeto, sat up a little taller in his perfectly tailored suit. "Yes, it appears I've discovered another one in Tokyo, Japan, linked to a most interesting—"

"That's enough, Moonshae!" Darcy yelled as he stood, pulling out the gun and pointing it at Moonshae. "I'm tired of your stupid, crazy obsession with these stones. It's time for new leadership."

Darcy squeezed the trigger. The bullet exploded out of the gun. Everyone in the room rose, shouting.

Zerick Moonshae didn't flinch.

As he sat in his seat staring at Darcy, he raised his hand

and slowly lowered it, ushering everyone to stay calm and sit back down. And then he smiled at the assailant, who remained standing. The bullet was suspended just in front of Moonshae's heart. He reached up and plucked it from the air.

"Ouch! It's hot," he said as he tossed it to the side. "Darcy, when will you ever learn?"

The man with the gun stood with his mouth gaping wide open. "How did you…how did you, do that?" he muttered.

The boss spoke softly as he rubbed his burned hand, "Simple, really. Knowledge, Darcy. Knowledge. If you don't control knowledge, then you have nothing. Now you must serve as an example." Moonshae pushed a button on his cane and a blue force field surrounded Darcy.

The man dropped his gun and everyone saw him start pounding on the walls of the force field, but no one could hear him. Then it moved and lifted him and his gun toward a door at the end of the room.

"Dr. Moonshae, please!" Kwame pleaded as he stood up, but the well-dressed man in white only looked forward at Darcy. Zerick Moonshae raised his finger at Kwame and then lowered it, as Kwame sat back down in his seat. The lights in the room lowered and the crescent moon on the table glowed.

Darcy stood helpless next to the door, pushed there by the force field as the wood panels on either side of the door lowered. The inky blackness of space lay just beyond the windows.

Moonshae stood up. "Now friends, please observe," he

said as he pressed the left side of the mahogany table in front of him. Darcy pounded on the force field, screaming silently to everyone in the room.

Dr. Zerick Moonshae cleared his throat. "You are all criminals and I own each of you," he said. "Your secrets are mine and so is your knowledge. If you cross me, there is not a hope for you or your family." He pressed the right side of the table. Holographic pictures began to float, spinning above the table, like baseball cards—they featured Darcy's entire family, all the way down his family line to his second cousins.

"I do detest violence," Zerick said. "But when it comes to matters of the mind, all of you can expect equal treatment." At the same time, across every one of Darcy's holographic family cards, a red slash appeared.

Moonshae looked at Darcy, who had stopped pounding on the force field and now was crying. The door opened and sucked the man directly out into the dead cold of outer space, away from the craft. Dr. Zerick Moonshae felt no remorse for Darcy, only marvel at his orbital supersonic jet that could convert to a rocket to achieve space flight. The door to the outer hull closed and the blue force field disappeared.

Moonshae sat down. "Now that I have your attention, let me remind you never to call me crazy."

11

Alpha287

Three long days passed at the CIA prep-school mansion and tensions were high.

Al tried to reason out more about his parents with Turnkey, but that quickly came to an end. Somehow, rumors had begun among the Trainees that Al and Turnkey had both failed the Agent Trials. To dispel them, Al admitted his failure in the cafeteria to everyone, but said Turnkey voluntarily stuck with the U.S.A., giving up Langley and the fast-track to becoming CIA Director. The announcement started an even more vicious rumor mill—wherever the two went at the mansion, whispers followed them.

Turnkey slumped on the bench next to Mary-Anne. "Everything seems so small and insignificant now. Even when we did the jump yesterday in the abandoned elevator shaft, all I could think about was how I gave up the chance to lead the CIA. Al is my brother, but I regret being so quick to give it all up. Maybe there was a different way."

Mary-Anne patted him on the knee. "Don't be hard on yourself, Turnkey. You made the right decision."

Turnkey took a bite of his apple as he watched some of the Trainees playing tennis. He shielded his eyes from the low afternoon sun as he turned to speak to her, but before he could say anything, Al came up from behind. "Hey guys. What's up?"

Turnkey gave a small smile. "Nothing much, yo."

Al looked at Mary-Anne. "Hey, you guys want to catch a movie tonight? We can grab one of the DVDs from the mansion library."

Mary-Anne smiled, but Turnkey looked down at the courts. "I don't know, man. I think maybe I'll just turn in early."

Mary-Anne looked at both of them and then smiled. "I'll watch something with you, Al."

Emerging from the mansion, a girl Trainee ran over to the agents. She had long dark hair. "Hey, the Chief wants to see you three in his office right now."

"Sure thing, Meghan. We'll come right now. Let's go, boys."

~

Mary-Anne knocked.

From behind the wood door, they heard the Chief's voice, "Come."

The three agents walked into the huge mahogany paneled office. The Chief read books, lots of them, and the walls were covered in volumes. A huge oak desk stood in front of them, even bigger than the one in the skyscraper office.

The Chief looked upset. "Sit down, Agents."

They took seats in the red high-back chairs in front of the desk.

The large man gestured with his hand at Al and Turnkey. "Now that I've promoted each of you to Assistant Agent, it's time for you to move out of simulated missions. I just received a call from a good friend in Japan. One of his swords was stolen last night from his personal museum. He doesn't trust the local authorities because crime bosses have infiltrated the police. So I agreed to send you to Japan to investigate."

Al and Turnkey looked at each other and smiled.

They both turned to look at Mary-Anne but the Chief tapped hard on the oak desk, drawing their attention to him. He glared. "Don't let your excitement impair your judgment, Agents. This mission will be run like simulated ones from HQ and Master Xu will take point on Yellow Level. This may be a pushover mission, but you will treat it professionally, so gather your standard equipment and go to HQ. I'm taking the helicopter there now with Mary-Anne to prep. I'll have a van ordered ready in 2 hours to take you. This mission may be for a friend, but everything will be run by the numbers from HQ. If you screw this up, I will have your heads. Do I make myself clear?"

"Yes, sir," Turnkey answered for them.

~

Al was glad to get away from the rumor-mill of the mansion. The two agents talked during the quick ride into Manhattan about what they expected from the mission and Turnkey shared a little bit about his past experience in Tokyo.

They arrived at the Universal Sports Academy tower and entered. Pressing the elevator button for number 12, the doors opened. Turnkey and Al stepped into the HQ elevator and the doors closed.

"I.D. card please," said the familiar female voice in the closed elevator.

After the full laser scan the elevator spoke. "Welcome back, Agent Keystone and Agent Dangermond. You are instructed to proceed to the Briefing Room on Yellow Level."

The elevator dropped quickly and then slowed to a halt. The doors opened, "Welcome to Yellow, please watch your step." Each floor in the secret underground U.S.A. was color-coded and along the walls in the hallways was painted a thick line of that color.

The first underground level, Violet, sat 600 feet below the New York City surface and was buffeted by encased steel and concrete to keep any river or ocean water from Long Island Sound waterway out of the elevator and HQ floors.

Each level was about 20 feet below the next, which put Al and Turnkey about 700 feet below Manhattan.

The facilities mimicked CIA operations at Langley. The Chief had the levels built for Assistant Agents to do simple missions. Operations from HQ were pushover kinds designed to give Assistant Agents field experience before they left the U.S.A. The CIA decided to pump money into the program because the U.S.A. cranked out the best field operatives due to their early childhood education.

Al and Turnkey stepped out of the elevator and proceeded down the yellow-streaked hall to the BR.

Al gestured back to the elevator. "I wonder if I will ever meet the person whose voice speaks to us in the elevator?" He let out a large yawn. "I think if I were having trouble sleeping, I could have her talk me to sleep."

Turnkey smiled. "Everybody knows you have no trouble sleeping, Al. Isn't your record, like…19 hours straight, homie?" Turnkey nudged him with an elbow.

Coming to the end of the hall, the agents approached the thick glass door with the emblem U.S.A. and words *Briefing Room* etched on the glass.

The Briefing Room was large with sound-proof exterior glass panes. Along the glass walls, flat-panel monitors hung everywhere. Al loved to touch them and review different mission data as a Junior Agent. The room was dominated by the large oval yellow pine meeting table that surrounded a contraption in the center. Al didn't recognize it. The machine had an array of different light sensors on a supported metal ring in the shape of a volcano. In the center of the "volcano" was a thick mirror and a lens pointed directly toward the ceiling.

"Seats, everyone!" demanded the Chief.

Al and Turnkey and four others, including the Chief, sat down in the comfortable yellow chairs on rollers and pulled up to the meeting table. Among the six people were two Trainees that Al knew, Meghan and Xander. Perkins stood near the corner of the room, next to a plate of warm cookies wafting their delicious scent from a plate. Al nudged Turnkey and gestured toward the counter, just behind him.

The Chief stood up. "Welcome. This is mission Alpha287. Now that I have lost all my Assistant Agents to the CIA, except for Agents Keystone and Dangermond, I am allowing Trainees who have earned high marks to join us on missions operations. As you know, our motto is to *Silently save the world, one person at a time.* Everyone will hear of our failures if they occur, but no one hears of our successes, except us. I expect this to be run by the books. Am I clear?"

The Chief looked around the room and sat down. "Perkins."

"Yes, sir. Here is your tea, sir." Perkins put the teacup down in front of him. Everyone knew the Chief always drank Earl Grey. After a few sips from the hot drink the Chief turned to his right and called on his Chief of Staff. "Chin Chin, why don't you take over?"

Sensei Chin Chin Xu stood up from his seat. With a serene nod, the short, old Chinese man with a long white braided beard moved over to a set of buttons on the pine table. He pushed two buttons and the room darkened while the volcano machine in the center roared into action.

Above the center of the machine rose a transparent, holographic display of the earth. Al could see right through it. It was huge and beautiful—a visualization of the whole world.

With his high-pitched voice, the Chief of Staff began the briefing. "Today we focus on downtown Tokyo, Japan."

The holographic display inverted and zoomed down into the city of Tokyo. It rotated into a flat holographic 3D section of the downtown. Al had never seen anything like it. It included all the buildings, live traffic, and even showed the movement of people as dots.

Chin Chin looked at Mary-Anne. "Thanks to Agent Martinez's modifications, we now have the ability to resolve a level of detail unmatched in the world." Everyone in the room clapped and Mary-Anne blushed. Sensei Xu waited until everyone finished clapping to continue.

The Tokyo display zoomed onto one specific building. "Here at the Shinjuku Tower, Mr. Fudosan has lost his dearest possession."

The holographic display showed the building statistics of height, floors, and occupancy and zoomed to the upper levels of the building. It rotated slightly to reveal part of the interior of the top floors.

The Chinese man pushed a button and the room lights slowly brightened. "Sometime this morning New York City time, Mr. Fudosan reported that his antique, the Serpent's Blade, was stolen—the sword of the famous Viking King

Olaf Tryggvason. We know that Mr. Fudosan spared no expense to protect his family heirloom and all the rest of his treasures. He is very wealthy and his security system is well known to be impossible to crack."

Turnkey whispered to Al. "I'm sure Mary-Anne could hack it with her eyes blindfolded!"

Chin Chin looked at the Assistant Agents. "Agents Keystone and Dangermond will proceed to Japan to investigate the break-in, find out who stole the sword and report back to Headquarters. The thief remains veiled in a garment of black, protected by the night—identify the thief and we may recover the sword. As standard mission procedure, you will report to Agent Mary-Anne Martinez for further mission equipment. Are there any questions?" Chin Chin looked around the table. No one spoke.

"Good hunting, then."

Everyone got up from the table.

The Chief put down his teacup. "Agents. Stay in touch. I don't want you making major decisions on your own during your first mission as Assistant Agents."

"No problem, Chief. We'll stick to the plan," Al said as he gave the Chief a wink and took one of Mary-Anne's famous cookies from the corner table. He handed two cookies to Turnkey, who gratefully received them.

"Hmph! Get out of here! Your plane leaves in 90 minutes," he yelled.

Turnkey and Al left the room quickly to go to Blue Level.

Al shrugged his shoulders and laughed. "What did I say?"

12

Hidden Gems

Wondrous secrets filled Blue Level and it was Al's favorite place to be, other than rock-climbing a cliff. The entire floor was dedicated to Mary-Anne's research and her lab was enormous.

"Welcome to Blue Level. Please watch your step." Al loved that soothing elevator voice. All three stepped out.

The thick glass doors to her lab had a thumbprint scanner next to them. Turnkey reached out and twisted the locked handle and then remembered only the scanner could open it. He moved over to have his thumb scanned, but Mary-Anne cut him off. "Oh, I'll get it Turnkey."

She reached for the door handle, then turned and opened it for the guys to walk through.

"Hey, how did you do that? You skipped the thumbprint scanner," Turnkey said.

Mary-Anne smiled. "Oh, you know, I just have the magic touch." The guys looked at each other and shrugged.

The lab was an expansive room with a blue streak

running all the way around it on the walls. Flat-panel monitors were mounted everywhere. Gadgets and mysterious devices sat on top of tables, along with piles of tools and wires. Al wanted to touch them all.

Along the back wall of the lab, a set of vault doors stood closed and locked. Three kinds of stations were set up throughout the lab for construction, testing, and analysis. Bright lights illuminated the whole place. Mary-Anne went to a computer touch-screen and started typing while Al and Turnkey made their way to a table nearby.

Mary-Anne looked away from the screen toward Al, who was about to pick up a pen. "Don't touch that, Al!"

He froze. "What is it?"

"Oh, it's a special writing pen," she said.

"But what does it do?"

She laughed. "Well…it writes, silly!"

Picking up the pen, she showed him three small marks on the side of it. "Here. When you click the pen, it comes out of the casing so you can write with it. But if you twist the top of it to this mark and click the pen again, a small dart shoots out and can stun your enemy—there are three darts in there. Twisting to the second mark makes the pen turn red hot, enough to melt through metal. And if you twist to the third mark and wait for 10 seconds, the pen will act as a small explosive with the power of dynamite, but without all the fire," she said with a smile.

Al looked closer at the pen. "Whoa, Mary-Anne, can we have that for this mission?"

"Sure, Al." She opened a drawer to the table and inside

were about fifty of the same kind of pen. "Do you want one or two?"

The guys laughed and, each taking two, tucked the pens away in their pockets.

Al pointed to the other side of the room where a huge weight was suspended from the ceiling by a thin rope. "What's that?"

Mary-Anne walked over to the rope. "That's a new kind of strength cord I created. It can hold 4000 pounds of weight. It's made of Kevlar, making it bullet proof. If you step back here, guys, and put on these safety glasses, I'll show you."

Moving back to a platform that had a semi-automatic weapon about 10 feet from the hanging rope, she flipped a couple of buttons. Instantly there was a sound dampening field surrounding the three people. A red warning light began to flash around them. Mary-Anne pushed another button and the semi-automatic weapon began firing bullets rapidly at the cord, hitting it multiple times and ricocheting off it, sending the bullets into special foam walls off to the sides. The rope held.

She pressed another button and a huge flame sprayed at the cord. The flamethrower had no effect on it. Mary-Anne flipped it off and pushed the last button. Out shot an intense spray of liquid nitrogen, completely freezing it.

She turned off the spray and the sound dampening field. Mary-Anne grabbed a hammer from the table nearby and struck the cord as hard as she could, which shattered the ice on it but left the rope completely intact.

"It's resistant to freezing down to -196 degrees Celsius."

Al ran his fingers through his mussy blond hair. "Whoa! That's sport'n."

Mary-Anne smiled. "Thanks, Al. I haven't tried it yet, but why don't you or Turnkey see if the laser in your watch can cut the cord?"

Turnkey pulled back his sleeve. "Yo, step back." He pointed his watch toward the cord. Using the display on his watch to target the cord, Turnkey activated the laser and the beam shot from his watch. It was a direct hit, but the cord held.

"As I expected," she said. "It's tough stuff!"

Moving over to a drawer she pulled out a bundled Kevlar rope and handed it to the guys. "Here, this should be handy for you."

Al was surprised at its light weight. "What else do you have in mind for this mission that we can use, other than standard issue?"

Putting down her safety glasses and turning off the red warning light, she spoke to no one in particular. "Tee, I need some help."

"Yes, Mary-Anne. How can I be of assistance?" the computerized voice said. Tee was the artificial intelligence computer program she had created to aid her gadget creations in the lab.

Al had learned on previous visits that Mary-Anne's dad created the first few versions of the A.I. at his lab in Palo Alto, California. Mary-Anne perfected the A.I. at HQ. Tee had access to every technical plan, construction plan, and electrical engineering document publically available around the world and more than a few top secret documents owned by the United States.

Mary-Anne looked toward her computer touch-screen. "Alabaster and Turnkey are on mission Alpha287. Can you access the files for the mission and recommend any resources we have here in the lab?"

Tee quickly replied, "Yes, Mary-Anne. Resources 5-445 and 9-16 each have a high probability of aiding these agents on the mission."

"Ah, okay. Vault 5 and Vault 9. Got it, thanks!"

Walking over to the metal door of Vault 5, she spun the handle and pulled it open. The huge 8000-pound vault door opened to reveal a small room. There were many drawers of various sizes and Al wondered how many hundreds of gadgets must be hidden inside those drawers.

Mary-Anne punched in a security code inside the vault to unlock the drawers and then looked around the room. "Tee, which drawer was it?"

"Drawer 445," said Tee.

"Thanks, Tee," Mary-Anne opened the drawer marked 445. "Oh, yes! Of course!"

She pulled out a special garment of sheer black and walked over to a table in the center of the small room, spreading out the suit.

Mary-Anne looked at Al and Turnkey. "I call this the Chameleon Pannus. See, here on the back is the power source. It uses my standard electrochemical power—Amber Alchemy."

Amber Alchemy, or AA, was created by Mary-Anne and it was a power source that used highly concentrated chemicals in small amounts to generate a large supply of electrical power.

Al knew she was always trying to improve the output of power from AA since gadgets often required significantly more power than batteries could supply.

Al ran his fingers over the suit. "So it only has one use, like the Impact Suit when we jump in the elevator shaft?"

"Yep! So please use it wisely. I'm still working on making AA last longer. This cloth has built in sensors that register the colors around it and adapt to match them. So it hides you like a chameleon and makes you invisible. It will continue to quickly adapt to your surroundings to keep you essentially invisible for about 30 minutes. If you stand still, no one can see you. But after that 30 minutes… it's just a black suit."

Turnkey whistled. "Wow, Mary-Anne, that is incredible."

Al was impressed too. "So sport'n."

"Thanks! I really—"

Perkins barged into the vault, bursting on the scene. "Agents Keystone and Dangermond, you are scheduled to fly to Tokyo on our jet in less than one hour. The Chief informed me you need to go now." Perkins looked down at his clipboard.

Turnkey frowned. "Ah, man, okay. But what about Vault 9?"

"Tee, can you have two of item 9-16 put in crates and loaded onto the jet for Al and Turnkey?"

"Yes, Mary-Anne," said the computerized voice.

Al raised his eyebrows. "So, what is 9-16?"

She winked. "I'll just leave that for a surprise."

13

Speed

Al slept well that night on the jet. He and Turnkey each had their own rooms on the international flight. The U.S.A. spared no expense on the successful completion of clandestine missions.

Al heard three knocks on his door and a woman say, "Time to wake up. We land in one hour."

"Thanks," Al said through the door. He had already awoken himself a minute before the knocks. Even though he continued to think about the mystery of his parents when given the chance, Al felt better than he had in a long time.

He got up and prepared for the arrival into Tokyo. After putting on his clothes he went through his checklist of standard issue gadgets. Laser-watch. *Check*. Electro-pistol. *Check*. Lock-pick tools with pocket knife. *Check*. High-beam pocket flashlight. *Check.* He was especially excited to wear his pistol—the perks of being an Assistant Agent.

He stepped out of the room and went to the common cabin. Turnkey arrived after a while and the two sat, looking through the jet windows at the distant city of Tokyo. It didn't take long to land and the touch-down was smooth and easy.

"Welcome to Tokyo. The time is 10:22 AM and we have a mighty fine Japanese morn'n," came over the speakers from the cockpit. "Hope y'all had a pleasant sleep and flight with us." Because they were a private jet, airport-control directed them toward a specific aircraft hangar bay. The U.S.A. had special privileges for immigration and could bypass customs, directly.

"When we reach the hangar, y'all sit tight. We'll have to unload some large crates from the cargo hold that will take a little extra time," said the captain. "Jill, can you call ahead and have those boys in the hangar ready to unload the crates as quick as they can? Over and out."

Once the plane stopped in the hangar, Al could see the ground crew move to unload the storage compartment. Al and Turnkey grabbed their backpacks, looked at each other, and with a double-bump of their fists, they deboarded the jet. Stepping down the stairs to the hangar floor, they saw the crate box tops being lifted off their bases—underneath, two high-powered motorcycles.

Al stood motionless. "Is that what I think it is?"

Turnkey pointed his finger. "Yo, the crate has 9-16 written on it. That has to be from Mary-Anne's vault."

They ran over to the bikes.

Al moved his hand along the lines of the motorcycle and whistled. "So, I guess we aren't using a standard car for this mission?"

Turnkey looked over at Alabaster and smiled. "Nah, man, looks like since you've passed Advanced Training on motorcycles like me, we get to ride in style. Now put on your brain bucket and let's get going."

Al had worked hard in the vehicle simulators as a Trainee. At thirteen, he practiced on a track with a motorcycle and just after his fourteenth birthday, he had passed advanced training. He felt prepared for anything.

When Al put on the black helmet with green flames, the face glass came to life. "Hello, Alabaster," the voice inside the helmet said. It was Mary-Anne. Her face could be seen on the inside of the helmet glass covering his face. "This is just a recording to get you acclimated to the motorcycle. This helmet is voice activated, so all you need to do is say the command, 'Okay Bike' and tell it what to do. Of course, if you prefer manual, you can just push the buttons and touch screen on the machine too. Tee and I have packed it with all sorts of extras." Al looked down at the body of the bike and saw it had a touch screen and several buttons.

Mary-Anne disappeared on the screen and a schematic of the motorcycle appeared on Al's helmet face but she continued to speak. "I've programmed the motorcycle to recognize only your thumbprint on the start-up button, so no one can start the bike except you or Turnkey. Just press the green button to get it started. There is a built-in high-res GPS to help you navigate. It will register everything in your helmet."

Al looked over at Turnkey, who was also listening on his helmet. "You can access forward and rear cables if you need assistance in high-speed turns, and if you are being followed, the oil slick, diamond stud tacks, and magnetic burners are standard." Al looked down to see the cable ports.

"Last thing is the turbolifter. If you are going at least 130 miles per hour and use the turbolifter, it will launch you into the air for at least 130 feet—you can adjust the height and distance exactly to your specifications. Just remember the number 130 and you'll be fine. Okay. That's about it… Oh, wait, I almost forgot! I've programmed the bike to have autopilot, so if you want that mode engaged it will drive itself at whatever speed you set. Signing off. Be safe!" Mary-Anne's voiced ended.

Al spoke into his helmet. "Turnkey, can you hear me? Did you get all of that?"

Turnkey nodded. "Yo, Mary-Anne never ceases to amaze!"

Al put his thumb on the green button and the motorcycle roared to life. Turnkey did the same and they revved the engines. Al looked down at the instrument panel. Manual control was located just below the handle bar on the main body, which also had a touch screen.

Al gave the computer helmet a try. "Okay Bike, route me to the Shinjuku Tower, downtown Tokyo." Inside Al's helmet, a digital map appeared on the glass with the whole route, and a voice began saying the directions.

Al looked over at his partner. "Ready, bro?"

"Yo, lead the way!"

They drove out of the hangar and onto the road. From there, they followed a series of narrow, short paved roads to navigate out of the international airport maze. As they neared the exit of the airport road system, they turned right to get onto the main roadway leading north along the western edge of Tokyo Bay. They passed two large black cars, which began to follow the motorcycles.

14

Dragon's Tail

TOKYO, JAPAN
35.677840 N, 139.758334 E

The two riders entered the freeway to travel north to downtown Tokyo on their sleek black motorcycles.

"Hey, Turnkey, my bike is amazing!" Al said as he revved his engine, rapidly accelerating up to the speed limit of 60 miles per hour.

Turnkey kept up with him and looked over. "Incredible, man. Hey, how long did the GPS say to the Shinjuku Tower?" The sound was crisp and clear in Al's helmet.

"About one hour."

Al saw Turnkey press something on his bike and then heard him in his helmet. "I hope we go by the Samurai statue in the Imperial Gardens just north of here. I saw it when I was here for a basketball tourney and it's huge." Al was about to comment when he noticed two black cars in his rearview mirror, speeding up right behind them.

"Whoa, do you see what I see?" Al said.

"Yeah, looks like we've got company. Let's speed up to 70 and see if they stay with us." They revved their motorcycles and sped ahead.

The onboard computer spoke into Al's helmet. "Warning. You are exceeding the speed limits." The black cars sped to keep pace with them. A red laser shot out from the first black car.

"Look out!" Al yelled. "They're targeting us with a laser sight!"

Both riders swerved to the left and right on the freeway and hit the throttle. Dodging from side to side, the riders moved in and out of cars on the road as the black vehicles rapidly pursued.

Al pressed a button near his ear to clear the breath condensing on the inside of his helmet glass. "Who are these guys?"

Turnkey looked back. "I don't know, but those look like gun turrets sticking out of the sides of the lead car." Al checked his mirror and saw them too.

The gun turrets from the front car unloaded a volley of bullets at the motorcycles.

"Evasive maneuvers!" Al shouted. The agents swerved out of the path of the shooting car and hit their throttles.

Al yelled into his helmet. "Okay Bike, release diamond stud tacks on my mark. Three. Two. One. Mark!" Out of the back of Al's motorcycle came several diamond-coated tacks sprawling across the road.

Al looked back and saw the black cars drive over them like they weren't even there. "They have reinforced tires!" He hit his throttle and the bike helmet showed 100 miles per hour. Al passed other cars in the blink of an eye but the black cars kept the pace. The lead car opened fire again, splaying bullets all over the road and hitting cars in their path. Al saw in his mirror the wake of bullet-riddled carnage left by the black cars as innocent drivers crashed into each other and the median on the highway.

Just ahead was a curve.

"Turnkey! Try the oil!"

"Yo!" A steady stream of oil hit the highway out of the back of TK's motorcycle as he went through the curve, leaning to the left to keep his balance. Al saw the lead black car send out a blue beam of high-intensity light from the bottom of the car and they drove through the oil slick, making the turn on the freeway with solid traction. Al had never seen anything like it before. He punched in the code to alert the local authorities of the danger. His motorcycle began to broadcast a secret signal the police could pick up to find them.

The pursuers were not slowing down. Al and Turnkey sped up out of range of the bullets.

"Warning! The freeway is ending," said the GPS. The bikes were entering the city streets of the downtown. The streets of Tokyo—the most populated city on earth—were always packed with cars and pedestrians through the whole megalopolis.

"TK, we've got to get away from these guys! There are more people downtown they will hit!" The motorcyclists took the off-ramp and banked hard to the right, but they were going too fast. Al slammed on the brakes and narrowly missed hitting the curb. The riders swerved around the cars sitting at the stoplight at the bottom of the ramp.

The black cars closed the gap and opened fire on the off-ramp, ripping into the two cars in their way.

Alabaster saw white streaks shoot past him as they skipped off the road and hit the buildings on the other side. Pedestrians scattered and ran for cover. "Whoa, what are those?"

Turnkey throttled past Al on the straight Tokyo street. "I don't know, but we have to stop these guys. Follow me to the gardens; I have an idea." Al looked back and saw the black cars blocked and slowly maneuvering around the two destroyed cars on the off-ramp. Al and Turnkey gained distance from them and Al could hear police sirens.

Alabaster turned off the annoying GPS that was constantly trying to re-route him to the Shinjuku Tower. He followed his partner on a northerly route toward the Imperial Gardens.

As they drove, Al looked back down the hilly road they were on and spotted the black cars still in pursuit. A police car drove onto the main drag from a side street, cutting off the second black car. The second car blew the Japanese police off the street with the white bullets. The lead car raced toward Al and Turnkey, while the other made its way through the debris left from the police car.

"TK, let's try the magnetic burners." The two riders slowed down significantly and Al looked directly at the first car.

"Okay Bike, ready magnetic burners!" The display on Al's interior facemask formed an auto-targeting cross hair. "Target confirmed," he said, and the computer zeroed in on the lead black car. "Geometry matched. Target acquired," said the bike.

"Launch magnetic burners!"

Four soup-can sized metal canisters launched from the back of Al's motorcycle into the air. The canisters flew down the street in a large arc, zooming past skyscraper buildings toward the first black car.

Al saw confirmation of the hit on his helmet screen. The canisters magnetized to the hood of the car and began to glow. The magnetic burners changed color from red-hot to a blinding white-hot. Then they disappeared into the heart of the vehicle.

The car made a hiccup, thrusted forward hard to the side, and then stopped. The burners had destroyed the engine.

"Yes!" Al pumped his fist.

The second car swerved around the disabled lead and kept pursuing the agents.

"Turnkey!"

Out of the back of Turnkey's motorcycle, four canisters shot out, arcing toward the second black car.

This time the pursuers were apparently paying attention.

They pointed their gun turrets up and shot the canisters, disabling them in mid-air. The canisters fell onto the road and rolled away on the pavement.

"Punch it!" Turnkey said into Al's helmet and the two riders took off toward the gardens. Winding their way through the streets they quickly made it to the high grass hedges, beautiful ponds, and cobblestone paths of the Imperial Gardens. An army of police sirens sounded in the distance.

The riders hit the cobbles and slowed down due to the difficult terrain on the pathways. The black car drove right up onto the cobbles but had no trouble with them, gaining on the motorcycles.

Turnkey shouted into Al's helmet, "We've got to get to the Samurai statue!"

Al drove behind TK, and the black car began to fire its white projectiles. The riders swerved to the right and took a narrow wooden bridge. The black car slowed to find an alternate route since it was too narrow.

Al saw several walking bridges ahead and, to the side, saw the black car heading to cut them off at the end of the bridges. In the distance was a huge statue of a Samurai on a horse.

Crossing the last walking bridge, the riders skidded onto the cobbled straightaway—and coming fast right behind them, the black car. The bullets started whizzing past the agents, but then stopped.

"They must be out of ammo!" Al shouted into his helmet.

The car closed in on them.

"They're trying to ram us!"

Turnkey pointed to the statue base ahead and yelled to Al through his helmet. Al pressed a button on his bike in response and a targeting computer display appeared on his helmet.

"Target acquired."

The black car thrust forward, about to hit Alabaster's back wheel, when Al gave the command, "Three. Two. One. Launch!"

A cable shot out of Al's motorcycle and grappled onto the base of the Samurai statue. Turnkey's bike did the same and they both made an arced turn to the left at 80 miles per hour with the support of their cables. As the black car tried to make the same turn, it lost balance, flipped over in the air three times and landed right into the water next to the statue.

The agents made the full turn, released the cable on command, and slowed to see the spectacular results.

Al took off his helmet. "Whoa! That was close!" The men were slowly emerging from the crushed car sitting in the shallow pond. They looked completely disoriented. "Who are those guys?"

Turnkey looked off into the distance toward a massive number of approaching sirens. "I don't know, man, but let's go to the tower. We'll use the video camera recordings from the bikes to see if Mary-Anne can ID these goons; we can let the local police capture them. We have to stay on mission."

Al put on his helmet and turned off his broadcast position for the police. "Okay Bike, forward all camera recordings from the last hour to Agent Mary-Anne Martinez for analysis and send a request to Agent Chin Chin Xu to connect with the local authorities about what happened. Over."

Alabaster let out a deep breath and opened and closed his hands several times to loosen them up—he hadn't realized the death grip he had had on his handle bars.

He revved his engine. "Let's go." The two agents drove off of the cobblestones and onto the street, toward the Shinjuku Tower to meet with Mr. Fudosan.

15

Konichiwa

Arriving at the Shinjuku Tower, the agents drove up to the canopy that overhung the main entrance and parked their motorcycles. Immediately, an entourage of young Japanese men briskly walked up to the agents as they put their helmets on the backs of their bikes.

Al put his hand on his Electro-pistol, strapped under his left arm inside his jacket.

All the men bowed in Japanese style. The best-dressed among them stepped forward. "Welcome to Tokyo, gentlemen. My name is Sota. I will escort you to meet Mr. Fudosan at the top of the tower." Al took his hand off the pistol and the two agents followed.

The entourage went in the main entrance and walked through the high-class lobby full of people meeting over business—some looked their way, but most ignored the group passing through. The lobby was full of fountains with orange Koi fish and the place had a modern, sleek look. Al wondered if they were in for more surprises, like on the road. He casually put his hand into his jacket.

The group stopped at the golden elevator doors on the other side of the lobby. The leader, Sota, took a key out of his pocket, inserted it into a slot, and turned it. Above the lock a small panel opened, revealing a hand-scanner. Sota put his hand in as three other men moved around to protect him. The scan finished and the elevator door opened.

"Please, come this way," Sota said, extending his right hand to beckon the secret agents into the elevator.

"Mr. Fudosan takes every reasonable precaution to limit access to his floors—this is one of two private elevators that ascends to the top. In a moment, I will introduce you to him and then we may begin the investigation."

The elevator door opened to the thirty-seventh floor and Sota stepped out. He removed his shoes and the agents did the same. Walking from the foyer, he led them through a series of sliding doors made of bamboo wood trim surrounding paper panels. The panels had ornate nature scenes drawn on them, accompanied by Japanese script. Al had never seen a place quite like this one before. After navigating the maze of doors, they arrived at the boss's office and went in.

"Gentlemen, please let me introduce Mr. Fudosan," the escort said.

Mr. Fudosan stood and approached the agents. "Konichiwa."

Turnkey and Al replied the same greeting by putting their hands to their side and bowing from their waist as they said *hello* in Japanese.

The man gestured to a picture of himself and the Chief from years ago. "Your boss, the Chief, has assured me that you have all the skills necessary to uncover the truth of my missing blade. I trust his judgment. Because I am allowing you security clearance to access my personal collection, I must be certain you are who you say you are." The elder man walked over to his desk. "Please put your eyes into this viewer for a retinal scan."

Al and Turnkey moved over to the desk and started the scan. Turnkey went first and the machine beeped—TK was cleared. Then Al put his face on the viewer. The machine sound was negative. Al looked around the room and shrugged his shoulders.

The old man frowned. "Please, try again." Al noticed the man move closer to a wall that had mounted katana swords.

Al gave another try, but it failed again. He could feel sweat forming on his forehead and he wondered what was wrong with the machine.

"Sota, help this agent," the boss said as he moved next to the wall of swords.

The Japanese escort made an adjustment and scanned Al again. This time the machine gave a beep. Al blew out a breath.

Sota looked over to his boss and the older man gave a

slow nod. "When you find my precious blade, do your best to apprehend the thief. I must know why my treasure has been taken. It has been in my family for a thousand years. I was told by my father only one thing about the Viking blade—to guard it with my life. I have never understood why Viking King Olaf's sword is worth my life, so you must bring me the thief. He stole nothing else."

They bowed to each other and Sota spoke, "Please follow me, agents."

~

The three went down one level to a place that looked like an artifact museum. Hundreds of knives and swords and suits of Samurai armor were on display. Al felt a sense of awe as Sota led them through the expansive collection of weapons in the darkened museum. The Japanese man assured them that this private, world-class museum was rarely seen by outsiders. They learned that ancient swords of the greatest Samurai were held here, purchased by Mr. Fudosan or passed down from ancestors.

Sota motioned to them. "Over here."

They approached a large, ornate structure that was different from the rest of the cases in the museum. It was round and made of wood, with a glass display case on top. It stood by itself—clearly, it was in a place of honor. "Here is the case where the Serpent's Blade was held," Sota said.

The ornate base was made of various kinds of wood. As Al circled the structure, he could see continuous carving wrapped all the way around it, illustrating a Viking sea battle.

The Japanese man pointed to one part of the battle scene. "Agent Dangermond, this depicts the final battle of King Olaf, when he was overwhelmed by his enemies on the sea. This ship is his, the Long Serpent. See here, the artist has carved him on the deck. That is the Serpent's Blade."

Al could see intricate details carved into the wood. He pointed to the depiction of the blade. "Does it look like this?"

Sota nodded. Al looked above the base into the empty large glass cover on top. A display stand sat inside on top of a red cloth, but no blade was present.

Sota lifted his hand to his chin. "As you can see, the case has not been broken. The seal is intact. The epoxy bead sealing the glass edges to the top is undisturbed. And I cannot find any cut in the glass. So the thief somehow had to steal the sword without breaking the seal."

He raised an eyebrow. "How could the Serpent's Blade be taken?"

Al looked closely at the glass case but saw no disturbance. He scratched his head, then looked at TK.

Turnkey turned to Sota. "Do you have lasers or video protecting this area?"

"Yes, there are lasers, but no video. At night in lock down, the invisible lasers rotate in a random pattern. A thief could not possibly navigate through the invisible laser field. On the ground, do you see the thin white line around the base? All the other cases have them too. The lasers shoot down from the ceiling and hit the floor but they do not pass the white lines."

Al looked up at the ceiling. "Did you find any anomalies with the laser system? Did it shut down for any amount of time?"

"No. The system diagnostics showed no inconsistencies. The lasers on this level were operating without problem."

Al looked up at the ceiling but saw nothing. He bent down to investigate the floor around the Serpent's Blade case.

Al knocked on the wood base but didn't hear anything out of place; he did the same to a few of the other cases in the hall to compare.

Turnkey looked closely at the empty case. "Maybe the thief came from the floor below?"

Sota shook his head. "Impossible."

"What's below this case?" Turnkey asked.

Sota shrugged his shoulders. "There is nothing. The 35th floor is empty and protected by a permanently installed laser grid. Mr. Fudosan keeps it empty as a protective buffer between the lower levels and his levels at the top of the building."

Al rubbed his hands together. "Well, let's go check it out."

16

Lots of Lasers

The elevator doors opened to a vast empty floor, clean and full of windows on every side. The elevator shaft was positioned near the center of the 35th level, so the elevator occupants could only see about half of the floor in front of them. Sunlight streamed in from the windows and laser canisters were mounted on the walls, but nothing appeared to be coming from them.

"Are the lasers on?" Turnkey inquired.

Sota nodded his head. "Yes. Do you see those green lights on the floor? If they are green, the lasers are on. If they are red, the lasers are off. Security personnel only need to open the elevator from here to see if things are operating properly."

Sota handed Turnkey some glasses. "Here, look for yourself."

Turnkey slipped on the glasses. "Yo! The canisters are shooting out a laser net, hovering just above the floor from the walls. That's cool. Nobody could tiptoe through that."

Turnkey handed Al the glasses to try them out. He looked to the outer windows and saw lasers near the windows were vertical, creating protection even from window break-ins. "Yeah, this place is locked down with lasers everywhere."

Alabaster looked at Sota. "How do you turn them off?"

"With this panel right here," Sota said, as the three peeked out of the elevator and looked to the side.

The Japanese man pointed to the panel. "It requires a hand scan and code entry. See that line on the floor? Don't pass it or the alarms will go off."

Al saw the line extended just outside the elevator with room enough for one person to access the scanner.

Sota stepped out of the elevator and put his hand on the scanner and punched in a code. The green lights on the floor went red. The laser security net was off.

Using a digital map of the building's architectural plans on a touchscreen tablet, the three made their way from the elevator over to the spot just below the location where the case was situated, one level up.

Al pointed up. "Do you see that?" There was a hole in the ceiling. "Sota, is that supposed to be there?"

The Japanese man looked shocked. "No. How did that happen?"

Al put down his backpack and took out his flashlight. "It looks big enough for a thin person to fit through. Boost me up, Turnkey."

Turnkey cupped his hands and hoisted the agent up to

the hole. Al stepped up onto Turnkey's broad shoulders while he poked into the hole with his flashlight.

"Yep, it looks like the thief accessed the next floor through the ceiling. There's a crawl space between the levels up here and I can see the remains of the ceiling scattered up here.

"See anything else?" Sota asked.

"Oh, man. Looks like the thief used a laser to get right into the base cabinet for the sword. There's a nice big hole in here and it looks like he must have cut the metal plate on which the sword and glass case sit. I bet he lowered it down into this crawl space and welded the metal back into place… The glass seal never had to be broken."

"See anything else, yo—like a sword?" Turnkey laughed.

"I wish."

Al stuck his head out of the hole and Sota looked at Turnkey. "Well, if the thief stole the sword this way, how did the alarms fail to go off? We have had no indication of a system shut-down. And my security forces use these infrared glasses when they open the elevator doors. They've seen no change in the green light status or failure of the laser net."

Al looked around the crawl space with his flashlight again. "From the looks of this job, the guy is a pretty resourceful person."

"And how did the thief escape?" Turnkey asked as he looked up. "Does the crawl space go far, Al?"

Al poked his head back out of the hole. "No, man. It looks way too tight up here to get through the space."

Sota sighed. "Who could have stolen the blade with such precision and then just disappeared?"

"I did," said a voice near the elevator. Al looked down through the ceiling hole and saw Turnkey and Sota turn around toward the elevator. He poked his head out of the hole to see a person in black clothing from head to toe, pointing a gun right at them.

"Sorry I can't stay and chat, boys." The intruder pressed the button on the wall, the elevator doors opened, and she got in.

As the elevator doors closed, they could hear her laughter, "Ha, ha, ha, catch you on the flip side."

The girl was gone. And sitting on her back—the Serpent's Blade.

17

Eagle

Al watched as Turnkey and Sota bolted for the elevator.

"Hey, wait! Help me down!" Al shouted as he shimmied himself out of the hole. Turnkey went back and helped him to the floor. Al grabbed his backpack and they ran to the elevator.

Sota was at the hand scanner and had just finished typing something.

Al looked at him. "What did you do?"

"I shut down the elevator system and locked down the building."

Almost as soon as Sota finished speaking, Alabaster heard locks engage somewhere on their level. The alarm began to blare.

Sota spoke something Japanese into a small microphone on the hand scanner and then shouted toward Al and Turnkey, "I told my men about the security breach and to start searching from the ground floor for a thief in black with the stolen sword."

At the same moment, two beeps chirped from Al's watch. His screen identified the caller—it was Mary-Anne. Al let the communication link come through.

"Al—"

"Hi, Mary-Anne, this isn't a good time." Al turned away and tried to listen to Turnkey talking to Sota about the elevator.

"Al?" she asked.

He pulled the watch closer to hear her speak. "Listen, call me back when the alarms stop blaring. Those guys that attacked you on the streets are not small time. They're part of a criminal ring—"

"Mary-Anne, I gotta go, we just spotted the thief! Talk soon." Al pressed the end button on his watch.

Turnkey grabbed Al on one shoulder, "Yo, man, you shoulda heard her out. We've gotta listen to HQ if they have intel for us." He paused and let go of his shoulder. "Don't worry about it now."

Turnkey turned back to Sota. "We gotta get access to this elevator. Can the scanner do it?"

"No. The elevators are shut off during security lock down. The thief is probably stuck between floors somewhere down in the shaft."

Al looked around. He wanted to cover his ears to block the pounding sound bouncing off the concrete floor. "Is there any other way off the floor?"

Sota pointed and they ran toward the stairwell door on the opposite side of the room.

As they went around the elevator shaft, Turnkey stopped,

followed by the other two. On the other side of the elevator, they found the equipment left by the thief and the location she had been hiding when they entered the floor. A series of ropes and belts hung from the ceiling and clearly the thief had been hanging out, literally, above the laser net the whole time.

Sota dug his hand into his pocket. "Wait! Here—I have a manual elevator key!" The man pulled out the elevator chuck and showed it to them.

They ran back to the elevator and Sota twisted the chuck into the slot to unlock the doors.

"Al, did you hear that thief's voice was a girl?" Turnkey said.

Al nodded. "That thief is a girl for sure. She's sport'n some pretty impressive skills to pull this off."

Turnkey nudged the doors open. "We gotta find her and get that sword back."

A huge rush of air rocketed out of the shaft, almost knocking Al down.

He regained his balance as the room adjusted to the air pressure difference. He helped Turnkey push the elevator doors fully open.

Al looked down into the shaft to find the elevator the thief took to escape. There was no elevator to be seen—it must have been a long way down.

Al looked at Turnkey. "Can we use the Kevlar rope to descend? Is there a place to tie it off?"

They looked up into the shaft. Al saw the elevator and pointed at it—it had gone up, not down.

"Oh, no. The roof!" Sota said.

Out of the corner of his eye, Al saw a dark shape soar past the window, outside of the building. "No way!"

He ran over to the 10-foot-tall window. The two others followed.

Out of the window, he saw the girl in black as she flew away. She wore a flying suit, which had small ballooning parachute air-catchers stitched between the legs and sides from hand-to-foot. She looked like a soaring eagle as she extended her arms and legs. Al had seen this kind of base jumping suit before. On some of his rock-climbing expeditions, people would jump off the top of the wall and glide down to the ground using a similar suit. They controlled the descent by angling their limbs, but Al always thought they were crazy to do it at such a low height. As he watched, he thought she looked like a superhero soaring through the sky of Tokyo.

The longer the trio watched her through the window, the farther she got from the building. She disappeared behind a skyscraper, no longer to be seen.

Al pointed in her direction. "Is there somewhere over there she could land? Like a field or a park?"

"Yes. The Yoyogi Park is that direction," Sota said.

Turnkey waved his hand to get Sota back to the elevator, "Shut off these blaring alarms and release the building lock down. We have to get to our motorcycles."

18

Dances of Mist

YOYOGI PARK, TOKYO
35.672070 N, 139.694605 E

Al and Turnkey reached their motorcycles parked at the tower canopy. Al jumped on and pressed his thumb to the starter, twisting the throttle to rev his engine. "Okay Bike, route to Yoyogi Park." The GPS said it was 12 minutes away.

The two riders zoomed down a series of streets. On the way, Al asked his bike to calculate the most likely landing location in the park for a base-jump off the top of the Shinjuku Tower. The computer told him there were two large open areas in the park, but a higher probability for a landing at the southern location, since it was bigger.

Coming off the street, the boys drove up onto the park sidewalk to get to the southern destination, since they had no direct street access from the north. People on the park sidewalk jumped out of their way as they drove past into the heart of the greenspace.

When they reached the southern opening in the forest, Al and Turnkey parked next to a bicycle rack. A large park sign was there and showed the field was once used as an Olympic Village for athletes in the 1960 Tokyo Olympics. Al looked around at the vast open area and saw ponds for resting by and shrines to visit, but remnants of the village were long gone. The thief was nowhere in sight.

Al took out his Electro-pistol from his jacket and strapped it to his hip for quicker access. He put on his communication headgear and performed a comm-check with Turnkey. He felt a thrill of excitement. Al had trained long and hard for this moment. He looked at his partner and knew TK was thinking the same thing—this was their first real encounter using hand weapons.

Turnkey looked off in the direction of the forest across the open field. "If you have a shot, let's take her down. When she wakes from the electrical charge, we can interrogate her."

They began to search the area on foot.

Like most of Tokyo, there were many people in the park, too. Al knew he and Turnkey looked out of place in the park as they pursued the thief. Despite the odd looks from the Japanese locals, the guys kept a steady pace looking all around for any trace of her.

Turnkey spotted her first. "Al." He gestured two times in the direction of the trees.

"I see her," Al said.

They systematically moved from tree to tree, concealing their pursuit.

~

The thief saw them coming. In fact, she easily could have made the getaway but she *wanted* them to follow her. She had waited patiently for Sota's hand imprint on the scanner to make her escape from the tower using the elevator, and now she would do the same with these agents.

For every step the boys pursued, she remained in perfect control of how much ground she conceded to them.

~

Al thought she moved like smoke in the wind, difficult to see and track as she darted between trees. Her every footstep looked like she was floating on water as she neatly glided across the land, just like she did when she soared through the air. The pursuit was like a dance. For every move there was a countermove. Never once was she in the range of their weapons, but they gained ground on her.

Al saw her disappear into a large set of bushes. He felt hot from the pursuit and wondered if they could catch her. Something in his gut made him uneasy. He slowed his pursuit and approached the area with caution.

Turnkey whispered into the comm mic, "This seems too easy, yo."

"I know. She might have a trap set in those bushes. I'll

take point." Al moved forward, stepping slowly toward the bushes. He nodded his head once at the bush. "Cover me."

Turnkey stopped and lowered himself to the ground, pointing his pistol at the bushes as Alabaster moved to the exterior edge of the hedge. Al peered in and saw a small opening, but no sign of the thief. He could hear himself breathing into the comm gear. "Okay, going in."

He pushed through the bushes into the opening and found a small concrete bunker with a metal door. "Looks like a utility shed back here with a door. Proceeding to open."

"Nothing stirring out here, yo. Watch yourself, Al."

"Roger that." Al opened the door slowly, using the door to shield himself from any attack that might come from within. He peered inside. It was a small room with a bunch of wires and conduits.

Al radioed back. "Looks like a standard utility bunker for maintenance crews. The girl is gone."

Turnkey spoke to Al through the comm channel, "Look for panels. Is there a manhole cover you can go down?"

"Nope, nothing. Wait. There is something. It looks like a new lever among a bunch of older-looking equipment. It's out of place." Al holstered his gun.

Turnkey whispered back. "Don't pull it, man. I bet it's a trap."

"That thing a trap? Nah, the girl is on the run. She couldn't have set up this thing as a trap."

Al carefully looked around for any clue. There was nothing else out of place. The wires and conduits looked normal and there was nothing he could see that might be a door or panel where the thief might have escaped. There was no option except the new-looking handle.

Al readied his hand on the lever. "TK, I'm going to pull it. Standby…,"

"Wait for me Al, I'm coming."

…

…

"Al?"

"Al, are you there?"

"Al, come in."

…

…

Silence filled the comm channel. Alabaster Dangermond was gone.

19

Dragon Fodder

Turnkey rushed into the utility closet and found it exactly as Al had described, except no new handle. TK felt confused as he pounded on the walls to test them inside the small concrete closet. He looked closely and examined as much as he could before giving up in frustration.

He tried one more time to contact his friend. "Alabaster, can you hear me?"

Empty silence. Turnkey slapped his fist on his thigh in frustration.

He moved outside of the small structure and out of the bushes to get a clear view of the sky. Looking down at his wrist, he spoke into his watch, "Mary-Anne, come in."

The connection was established and Mary-Anne's voice came through. "Turnkey, what's happening? Al never called me back. I said I needed to talk to you guys ASAP. But it's been over an hour since we talked."

"Al is gone, Mary-Anne. I can't find him anywhere."

"I bet the Dragon's Lair has him, Turnkey!"

He wiped the sweat from his forehead and took a deep breath. "Who's that? No, no, wait. Can you check the tracking chip in Al's shoulder?"

Everyone in the U.S.A. had a Vitals Tracking chip in their shoulder. Turnkey hoped Al could be located with it, or at least they could see his vital signs. Most of the time HQ gave their agents privacy and didn't use the VT unless there was a reason. Now, they had a reason.

Turnkey rotated slightly to the left to shield from the sunlight as he looked at his watch. "It's probably a long shot, if he's underground."

Mary-Anne turned back to the screen to talk, "Turnkey, the VT doesn't show anything. If Al is underground, you're right that we won't be able to get a reading. We'll keep monitoring it. Master Xu has some intel for you."

The short Chinese sage appeared on the video feed with a stern face. "Agent Keystone, the shroud of mystery has thinned only by a hair. We have determined from the footage supplied from the motorcycle chase that the men work for the Dragon's Lair. Tosaka Heeto is the criminal boss who leads this organization. He is an especially nasty fellow with his fingerprints deep in the corruption of Tokyo. My research shows he is motivated by money and kills as often as he wants. If the Dragon's Lair has Dangermond, we have to find him as fast as possible or Al could be killed. I am deploying two senior agents from New York at once to assist you. You will remain lead but must wait until they arrive to locate Agent Dangermond. I will send you the op in a brief."

"Sir—"

"No, Agent. You must wait for the senior agents. That is an order."

Turnkey sighed.

The Chinese man looked to his left on the video toward Mary-Anne at work on the computer. "Agent Martinez determined from your motorcycle chase that the blue light from the black cars changed the chemical make-up of the oil and made the slick like driving through water. She also analyzed the spectral signatures of those white weapons and they were plasma bullets—tough as real metal bullets, but worse, because they keep burning once inside you. The Dragon's Lair possesses advanced weapons and you cannot underestimate them."

Turnkey scratched his head. "Sensei Xu, all of this was a trap. They knew we were coming with the chase, and all. Then the thief tricked Al and now he's gone."

The Chinese man squinted his eyes. "There, no doubt, is a hidden agenda. We must raise the curtain of the stage to see the play. The senior agents will arrive within the next 12 hours to help you find Tosaka Heeto. He operates the largest Sumo Wrestling facility in town. Find Heeto and you will find Dangermond."

～

Alabaster found himself in the dark. Pitch dark. He raised his hand in front of his face and couldn't see anything. He reached for his flashlight in his backpack and was struck across the jaw and knocked out.

~

Al awoke from his slumber with a bucket of cold water to the face. He sat with his hands tied behind his back on a wooden chair.

Another bucket of cold water hit his face.

"Wake up, you scum," said the ugly man with the empty bucket in hand.

The thief put her hand on the wall. "Tsk, Tsk. Your ways are so crude. My employer detests cruelty and prefers a more humane manner of questioning." The masked girl adjusted her position and Al saw a large black dragon surrounded by a ring of fire painted on the wall. Another wall held a bunch of katana blades.

"Well, *my* employer prefers pain, and I haven't even begun the questioning," the man said. "What do you think this is, girl? A hotel resort?"

"You Dragon's Lair crooks are all the same."

Dragon's Lair.

Al tried to reach for his watch but couldn't get it with the bindings so tight. He started to roll his wrists behind his back to loosen them up. Turning toward him, the Dragon's Lair interrogator snarled. "Okay, scum. What were you doing in that tower for Fudosan?"

He threw another bucket of cold water into Al's face. "Speak!"

Al yelled back as he motioned his head toward the thief. "What do you think I was doing? I was chasing *her*!"

"Okay, pretty boy, want to evade the questions? Where is the money—where is it?" The ugly man raised his hand to strike Al.

Alabaster looked right at him. "What are you talking about? What money?"

The man struck him in the jaw and laughed. "What money? What money. The millions Fudosan stole from my boss in Thailand, you scum! The girl here texted us to be on the lookout that you were delivering it to him. That's why we…uh…had our little run-in with you in the streets, until you disabled my car with those burning gadgets!"

Al twisted in the chair and spit out blood from his mouth. The bindings were loosening. "Look, bud, I don't know what you're talking about, and I don't know anything about your boss's money. I'm here to get that sword back."

The man hit Al again across the jaw with the back of his hand. "Don't lie to me, boy. Your young looks and American passport get money moving wherever Fudosan wants. I've seen other young foreigners working for him. Where's the money, punk?"

Spitting out more of the blood from his mouth, Al composed himself—his training, especially the martial arts, taught him how to take a hit. "Ask her, she's the thief. I've got nothing to say."

"Oh, yes, you do!" the man raised his hand and the thief grabbed his arm, displaying surprising strength for her size. "How about you give me a turn?" The man pulled his arm away in anger and backed into the corner for the moment, brewing and steaming.

Al kept working on the bindings behind his back as she approached. He'd have to take on both of them once he got his hands free.

Bending down toward Al, she whispered into his ear. "I know you know nothing of the money. I tricked them into thinking Fudosan stole their money and you were delivering it. Give me the answers I seek and I will get you out of here." She sounded young, maybe like she was fourteen or fifteen years old.

Al listened to the secret words as he stared at the fuming man across the room. *What does she want? Think.* It was hard to concentrate with his jaw throbbing. The thief whispered, "I want to know what you know about the blade? What has Fudosan told you?"

Al closed his eyes. He recalled his failure in the Agent Trials. It was like he was there again—he had to focus on the details in front of him. He couldn't let her trick him. *Why does she want to know that? Why is that information valuable to her?*

The ugly man shouted at the thief. "What are you saying there?"

"Sweet chocolate, friend. Sweet chocolate. Sweets get answers more than violent methods," she replied, quick and smooth. Backing away and looking at Al, she spoke aloud. "Do you know where the money is?"

While she spoke, he felt the bindings stretch until he could reach his watch. He clicked the button to start recording the interrogation, with his hands still tied behind his back. Al decided to play along and make himself valuable, to gain her trust. He might be able to escape with the sword if he could create a distraction. For now, he needed to be convincing.

He spit again. "Yes. I know where the money is."

"Where is it, scum?" the interrogator said as he stepped up to Al.

The thief looked right at the ugly man and stuck out her foot as he stepped forward. He tripped and tumbled right into Al. His large mass smacked into the agent, who went crashing over, flying off the wooden chair.

Al took the impact of the crash on his right shoulder and it began to throb. As he lay on the floor, Al hoped the impact would have loosened his bindings but his hands were still firmly tied behind his back. The scruffy man looked at Al and raised his eyebrows, then shook his head. He got up and brushed himself off with a laugh, looking at the thief.

"You're dead, little girl." He reached back and pulled out a hand gun tucked in his belt behind him. Before he could aim and shoot, she already had pulled the sword off her back.

In one giant swing from over her shoulder, she cut his pistol barrel clean off! The man's arm swung downward from the impact and he screamed as he stumbled backward, tripping over Al's body on the floor. Alabaster saw the thief sheath the blade onto her back as the man got up. Behind him on the floor, he heard the Dragon's Lair man throw the broken weapon to the side. Then the man hopped over Al and charged the girl.

He dove at her, but she was too quick and easily dodged the man's attack. As she rotated to the side, Al saw her push the man from behind and he crashed into the wall. The man hit it so hard, a couple of the swords fell off their mounts. The ugly man lay on the floor, knocked out cold.

Almost mesmerized by the odd beauty of the fight he had just witnessed, Al stood up. He clicked his laser and cut the bindings off his wrists.

The girl turned to face him and stepped forward. "Have **a** seat, Dangermond, I'm not finished with you, yet."

20

Pens & Needles

Tokyo, Japan
35.696701 N, 139.793426 E

Tosaka Heeto was ruthless, violent, and the meanest gangster in Tokyo. He was smart and cunning and nearly untouchable—the police had yet to link him to any crimes, even though they suspected he was involved in everything from illegal merchandising to explosives racketeering. Heeto was the boss of a championship Sumo wrestling arena and could be found there during big matches.

At the Tokyo safe house, Turnkey put down the intel report on the gangster. He felt sick to his stomach. His best friend could be killed by the gangster and he had to wait for the two senior agents to arrive. He looked at his watch—still 7 hours until they touched down in Japan. Turnkey picked up the intel report again and scoured it for any clues. He couldn't take it anymore. He *had* to go rescue his friend before the senior agents arrived.

Turnkey read through the operation brief Master Xu had sent earlier. He was supposed to go undercover to the Sumo arena, disguised as a millionaire of a technology start-up company. The operation, or op, was to make a request to meet with Heeto for a business deal. The brief said his goal was to obtain intel on Al's whereabouts from Heeto and, if possible, to get out with Al, aided by the senior agents acting as bodyguards.

He put on his nicest attire—a hand-tailored tuxedo, compliments of the agency. He checked himself in the mirror and adjusted his bowtie. He felt swank and smooth in these expensive clothes. Even though he was just fourteen, he looked at least eighteen, maybe nineteen. Knowing that Heeto might be expecting him, he altered his looks with fake eyebrows, a curly-haired wig to hide his short black hair, and glasses. He looked rich, important, and carefree. His agency course in *Disguise Techniques* served him well.

I'm coming for you Al.

He got on his motorcycle and drove in the direction of the Sumo facility. While he zoomed through the Tokyo streets his watch beeped. It was HQ. He piped it through to his helmet, audio only, so they wouldn't see his disguise and know he was disobeying orders.

"Agent Keystone, come in." It was Sensei Xu.

"Yo, Agent Keystone here, Master Xu." Turnkey slowed his bike down so HQ wouldn't hear him driving.

"Agent, are you on your motorcycle?"

"Yes, Sensei, I'm…uh…I just…I just couldn't stay still."
At least that was true.

"Yes, of course," Sensei Xu said. "I have an update. The senior agents I dispatched have had engine trouble and landed on Midway Island in the Pacific. They are fine, but another plane will not arrive to them for at least another ten hours. Therefore, they may not make it to you for another twenty-four."

"Twenty-four hours?"

"Yes, Agent. That is why I am sending you to meet Heeto without them. This is a dangerous op and you won't have senior agent backup. Don't underestimate Heeto. If he has Agent Dangermond and you can rescue him, make the attempt. But if you're in danger, get out of there. We don't want to lose two agents. The Chief and I have full confidence in you. Do you have any questions?"

Turnkey smiled. "No, sir."

"Remember your training. Good hunting. HQ, over and out."

The communication ended.

Whew. He was authorized.

After about twenty minutes of riding, he arrived near the arena district on his black motorcycle and parked a few blocks from the main complex, in case the Dragon's Lair goons were looking for his ride.

That night was a huge one in Tokyo Sumo competition. Sumo matches featured two massive, 400-pound men slamming their huge bellies into each other and trying to push one another out of a circle painted on the ground around them. The fans loved the matches—even if they were sometimes rigged.

Turnkey was supposed to request to meet with Heeto to discuss business. But the only way to get the attention of high-class criminals was to speak loudly—with money. Turnkey thought a huge bet on the premier match might get the attention of Tosaka Heeto and give him an audience with the crime boss. Besides, the U.S.A. safe houses always had a stash of money in case of emergencies.

"Put $300,000 on Tanaka defeating Yamota."

The Japanese ticket agent was not ready for such a large bet and it took him a little while to process it. He double-checked everything behind the betting window and gave the disguised secret agent his ticket.

Turnkey walked to his seat in the main arena where one of the lesser matches was already underway. The arena was a huge bowl with the seats rising up on all sides looking down into the bottom where the matches took place. Thousands of fans surrounded the main Sumo match platform in the center. At the top of the arena were the luxury suites. It was obvious which one held the gangster—the one that had all the huge thugs with weapons at their sides.

Several more minor matches were fought before it was time for the main event. The crowd erupted with applause as the premiere match was announced. People exchanged money around the arena, making personal bets on the big event.

Turnkey looked up and saw Tosaka Heeto emerge, sitting

in the lofty luxury box, front and center, watching the start of the big match.

Tanaka was the underdog and Yamota, the champion. The two huge warriors entered the battle circle. They each reached into a bag and pulled out a handful of something white, tossing it around the circle. Turnkey thought it looked like salt. Then they looked away from each other in a squat position as they lifted their thick legs, stomping them down. They slapped their arms on their chests and shook out their massive biceps. Tanaka looked much bigger than Yamota, but the champ looked stronger. Hearing the word, they turned and approached their start line in the circle, a few feet opposite one another. The large men bowed to the referee and then bowed to each other. The ref looked at them and then dropped his arm to start the match.

The men exploded forward with their huge bellies and the crowd roared. Tanaka's weight was obviously a surprise to Yamota, because the champion stumbled on impact. Yamota slapped his huge arms down on Tanaka's shoulders and the men began pushing and grabbing, using their weight to best advantage. The champ was smart and backed slightly away, forcing Tanaka forward and off-balance. Yamota grabbed him and turned to the side, using the momentum from the huge man to toss him to the edge. Like the early matches, it was over in less than a minute.

The U.S.A. agent had just lost $300,000.

Now, he had to wait to see if his wager got him in to see Heeto. As the main event ended and people began filing out of the arena, Turnkey stalled in his seat by looking at the warrior match card. When his row was empty, a very pretty woman in a red dress approached him. "Mr. Heeto would like to invite you to his luxury suite for an after-match meal and business proposition. Please follow me and I will show you the way."

Turnkey smiled. He followed the woman in red out of the arena and into a private elevator. She punched in a code on the elevator touch screen and it went up.

He turned to look at the woman. "A business proposition, you say? Well, this ought to be interesting."

She took him directly to Heeto's office, which was in the back of the luxury suite, away from the arena floor. There, the crime boss sat behind his huge wooden desk. Windows adorned one side that looked out into the large luxury box and thence into the arena. Turnkey thought the luxury box was more like a playground for the wealthy. There were beautiful tables, a bar for ordering drinks, fish tanks filled with exotic aquatic species, and even a small dance floor. Televisions lined the walls of the suite, playing Sumo matches and showing other sports from around the globe. Thugs stood guard all around.

Heeto stood up. "Welcome to my arena, Mr...?"

Turnkey bowed. "Name's Jones. Thomas Jones. And you are Mr. Heeto?"

Both men looked like millionaires but only one of them had an empire of crime. Heeto motioned to the disguised agent. "Please have a seat, Mr. Jones."

"Yes, I'm Tosaka Heeto, the owner of this Sumo facility. Would you care for some food? Perhaps some sushi?"

Turnkey nodded. "Ah, yes, that would be excellent!"

Heeto clapped his hands and one of his men left the room.

"Before we eat, do you mind if we discuss a business proposition? I could not help noticing you made a large bet this evening and I thought you—"

"Might like to get it back?" Turnkey chuckled aloud.

"Yes," Heeto said.

"Go on," the disguised agent said.

Heeto smiled at him. "Tell me, Mr. Jones, are you interested in Sumo enough to sponsor wrestlers? Wealthy young men like yourself are in need of something to do with their money. I can see from your clothes you are man of style. I can offer you a 2-for-1 return on your investment. For every $5 million invested, I guarantee $10 million back." The boss had other ways, criminal ways, to guarantee that kind of return and Turnkey had read about them.

"Well, that's quite a bit of money, now, isn't it?"

The Japanese man gave him a puzzled look. "Indeed, and what is your business, Mr. Jones?"

"My business? Fun and pleasure, of course." TK was enjoying the performance until he noticed a couple of small holes in the desk directly in front of him.

Barrels for bullets? Maybe poisoned darts?

The boss began to work on his computer at the desk. Turnkey thought he might be searching for his alias, Thomas Jones, so he gave a few more details to make sure the crime boss would find him on the Internet and see his millionaire status. Mary-Anne had set up a fake website so Turnkey would appear legitimate.

The agent noticed a clock on a side desk—the search was taking longer than it should. Turnkey squirmed in his seat. The Japanese man began to laugh a little.

"My Internet picture not so great?" He couldn't see the computer screen. Turnkey felt sweat forming on his forehead and wondered if his disguise was failing.

He looked again at the desk. Maybe those holes were some kind of x-ray device? His throat felt dry.

The crime boss kept his eyes on the computer screen. "Ah, nothing Mr. Jones, nothing at all."

Turnkey thought maybe his gig was up. He looked around the room and noticed through the glass a couple of guards out in the luxury box were whispering something to each other.

The crime lord turned and looked at Turnkey. "Fine. Fine. Tell me, do you like hot wasabi sauce with your sushi, Mr. Jones?"

Turnkey jumped back into acting mode and tried not to fidget in the comfortable chair. "Why, yes, yes, I do, Mr. Heeto. And how about green tea? You Japanese have the best green tea on the planet." As he finished speaking, the same two guards whispering earlier came thumping up just behind Turnkey. The short hairs on the back of his neck stood up and his shoulders tensed.

Heeto leaned down to get something from his desk drawer while he spoke. "Very good. Very good."

Turnkey looked down and rotated his wrist slightly to the left.

Sitting back up, the crime boss looked at the agent. "Very good, indeed. Now, before we eat there is one more thing I would like to discuss. Tell me, Mr. Jones, where is the money you and your pal, Dangermond, stole?" Heeto motioned for his men to secure the agent.

As the arms of the thugs crushed down on Turnkey, he launched out of his chair into a tucked position, rolling to the side of the desk.

The stunned guards reached into their jackets to pull out their weapons, but Turnkey was quicker and shot the men with Mary-Anne's pen. The darts dropped the huge men to the floor with a loud thump.

Mr. Heeto was slow to react and dropped to the other side of the desk. "Mr. Keystone. I am going to deliver a message to your boss Fudosan with your dead body. And after I kill you and your friend, Fudosan is next, unless I get my money."

Turnkey could hear at least a half-dozen men coming to the aid of their boss as he tucked himself close to the desk. He dared a quick peek and saw no one left beyond the glass, other than some well-dressed women who were uninterested in the happenings. He was trapped in the crime boss's office.

The Japanese crime lord chuckled as he cocked the gun in his hand. "This need not be violent… I'm a business man, after all. Come out and my men will not harm you. Just tell me where the money is that you stole for Fudosan."

Turnkey heard more men show up at the luxury suite. The stand-off was even more one-sided.

The gangster laughed louder at the trapped agent. "Come now. You are outnumbered 15 to 1. Surely even you do not discount those odds?"

There was only one way out of this mess. Turnkey grabbed the Electro-pistol out of his ankle holster and pushed the electric charge setting to max.

"No can do, Heeto! I want my partner back and you're going to give him to me!" As he finished, he twisted the top of Mary-Anne's pen, clicked it, and tossed it into the air from the side of the desk. It landed on the other side of the long room.

The large thugs laughed and one said in Japanese, "He thinks the pen is mightier than the sword!" All the men burst into a laughing roar.

Chaos erupted!

Just like Mary-Anne had said it would, the pen exploded with a large blast like dynamite. Turnkey heard the glass walls explode and the crushing sound of metal buckling as the groans of large men heaved into silence. A cloud of dust enveloped the desk and he waited patiently, listening for footsteps coming close. He gave a quick peek around the side of the desk toward the explosion.

Through the dust he saw a sea of large Japanese men stumbling about or lying on the ground hurt. Some were unconscious like beached whales, unable to move.

Taking a deep breath and letting it out slowly, Turnkey pointed his pistol around the edge of the desk and started shooting. The Electro-bullets hit the stunned guards one by one, and those left standing began to fall like dominos all around the room. Any movement in the room received an electro-stun from his gun. He did not see Tosaka Heeto, but Turnkey knew he was still there.

The agent yelled from the other side of the desk, "Well, yo, that just leaves the two of us, Mr. Heeto."

The Japanese man screamed in fuming anger, "You're a dead man!" A stream of white plasma bullets spit over Turnkey's head, riddling the wood panels opposite him. He could feel the huge oak desk shake from the pounding bullets, as splinters shot away in every direction, destroying all the television flat panels and various decorations on the walls.

Turnkey knew if he tried blind shots by pointing his gun over the top of the desk, his arm would get shot off, so he pressed hard against the oak side, hoping the plasma bullets would continue to get deflected. The smell of burnt wood soaked the atmosphere as the roar of the gun raged along with the Japanese crime boss.

Then the desk exploded! Turnkey flew into the air and slammed into the wall, landing prostrate on a pile of destroyed wood and electronics. He shook his head to recover from the blow and saw the fire from the x-ray machine inside the desk as it roared upward, setting off the water sprinklers.

The Japanese man shouted, "Stop!" He stood pointing his gun at Turnkey from across the room near the blown-out windows to the luxury box area overlooking the Sumo arena.

Turnkey stood up and raised his hands. "So this is how it is, Heeto? You just gonna blow me away and go on with business as usual?"

The man laughed at Turnkey, "So it would seem." Then he pulled the trigger.

The automatic weapon jammed.

Turnkey dove down for his Electro-pistol lying on the ground and popped up to find his target. Heeto had already discarded the weapon and was running toward the gun of the nearest guard.

"Freeze!"

Turnkey aimed his gun but Heeto didn't stop. The crime boss jumped over the rubble and the unconscious men lying about all over the place. Then, Turnkey unloaded his weapon.

Tosaka Heeto flew to the ground with a thud, completely knocked out from the Electro-pistol.

"Ah, man! Why'd you have to go and do that?" Turnkey said aloud to himself. "Now I've got to do it the hard way, yo."

Water from the sprinklers continued to spray as the fire from the desk smoldered. Destruction and debris surrounded the secret agent. He was the only one left standing.

Turnkey walked over to the boss, stepping over the chaos. Bending down, he searched the boss's pockets. He found several items, including a gold money clip that must have held several thousand dollars' worth of yen. But the most promising find was the small handheld smart phone of Tosaka Heeto.

Turnkey nodded his head. "That's right, dawg!"

Now he just had to access the entry code, which he had hoped a conscious Heeto would have been able to provide. Flipping a side panel on his watch, he pulled a small cord that extended from the base about two inches. It had a micro HD connector that plugged right into the smart phone. He started the algorithm on his watch that Mary-Anne had devised to break into locked phones.

Turnkey smiled, thinking of Mary-Anne. *She's the best*!

Tucking the phone up into his sleeve, he began to gather up all of the weapons he could see as the algorithm worked its magic. He threw the guns into the fish tanks still standing in the luxury area to neutralize the gunpowder with the water.

He found Heeto's weapon, which was still scorching hot, and saw the heat had fused the bullet chamber. The jam had saved his life. As he looked down at the broken weapon he heard a ding—the phone was hacked. He was in!

Accessing Tosaka Heeto's phone was like enrolling in a 'How to Be an Evil Boss' class at the university. The phone contained all the numbers and details of Heeto's criminal network.

For now, Turnkey was only interested in one thing—finding the elevator access codes to the boss's secret chambers. When he was in the elevator earlier coming up to the luxury suite, he had noticed there were many floor levels down below and guessed his partner was held somewhere beneath the arena.

Finally, codes in hand, Turnkey could begin his search for his friend.

21

Family Affair

Alabaster Dangermond stood in a defensive position. In front of him was the skilled and fast thief. He looked around the room for any advantages.

He saw:

A 20 x 20 foot room.

High ceiling with one hanging light.

Man on the ground knocked out.

One bucket and a tub of water.

A wood chair.

His backpack.

An array of swords on the wall.

One door behind the thief with the blade on her back.

He had to get the sword from her.

Al looked right at her masked face. "Who are you, and why am I here?"

The thief stood still in front of him. "Shut up, Dangermond. I'll ask the questions here. What do you know about the sword? How did Fudosan acquire it?"

Al needed intel from this girl, so he played along. "It's some Viking king treasure. It came from an ancestor. Didn't you know?"

"Don't play stupid, Dangermond. My boss wants to know how Fudosan got it. Tell me what you know."

Boss.

"Why does your boss want that info? Why not hack into Fudosan's system and steal it? You're a thief."

The girl laughed at him. "Yes, yes. Well, I've already done that and there is nothing there."

"Ah, well, sorry about that." Al looked at the swords lying on the floor next to the man knocked out.

The thief shook her finger from side to side. "Tsk, tsk, Dangermond. Don't make me hurt you, too. I'm the wind and the rain all in one. I'm everywhere and nowhere. Haven't you already figured that out? Tell me what Fudosan said about the blade."

Al looked beyond her at his backpack near the door. The swords were a better bet. "Tell me about your boss and I'll tell you what you want to know."

"Cute, Dangermond. Want his business card so he can hire you too? How about you shut up and tell me what I want to know?" The girl clenched her fists, ready to attack.

Al moved slightly toward the sword wall. "Does he pay

well? You obviously have some skill. Maybe we can pay better. It would be better than hanging with these Dragon's Lair goons."

She snorted. "Oh! He pays well. You could never match his money. What a funny thing. You can't offer me anything."

Al paused and looked right at her and spoke softly, "I can offer you freedom from crime."

"Shut up!" The thief's hands began to rotate in circular movements, like a snake ready to strike at any moment. Al thought he heard her sigh. A mask hid her face, but her sounds betrayed her—Al sensed she was wrestling with something.

A loud commotion from the door behind her distracted them and Al dove for the swords on the ground that had fallen when the thug smashed into the wall.

Grabbing two of the katana swords, Al stood up and faced the thief, swinging the swords so the sheaths flew off them. He held both swords pointed right at her, one sword high over his head and the other waist high.

She slowly reached over her shoulder and pulled the Viking sword from her back. "Well, Dangermond, you've got guts. I'll give you that. Since you seem to be silent on sword knowledge, how about you tell me the location of your parents' special stone?"

"What? My parents? *You* sent the email." Al launched his attack, jumping in the air right at her.

The thief crouched down by lowering one knee and raised the sword above her head, blocking both the katana blades as they crashed down on the Viking blade, sending sparks flying as metal struck metal. She swung one leg out to sweep Al and connected with one of his legs, causing him to stumble to the side.

Al yelled at her, "Why did you send that video of my parents' murder?"

"I didn't," she bit back.

Both stood with swords ready to slash. Loud bangs pounded outside the door, and the girl swung the ancient blade at Alabaster Dangermond.

He met her strike mid-air with one of the katana blades, one of the sparks coming close to his face.

Al swung the second blade at her legs and she jumped up as the sword flew underneath her. She pulled to the side and slammed the ancient sword down on the second blade, slicing it in half!

Al backed off and looked at the sword hilt in his hand. He threw it to the side, putting both hands on the handle of his remaining katana.

She jumped in the air to strike with her sword and Al parried with his blade. She crashed down on top of him and their blades pressed together.

Al shouted up at her. "Who do you work for?"

Face to face on the ground, he could see her dark eyes through the mask, and almost make out the outline of her face.

He pulled his knees up to throw her off, but she was too fast. She caught his knees with her feet and gave him an elbow to the jaw. She rolled off him to the side and flipped up onto her feet, with sword in hand, while he laid on the ground. Just as she reached into her pocket, a huge explosion burst the door open.

Turnkey stood in the doorway with his pistol drawn, ready to attack!

22

Trust

"Turnkey!" Al felt a wave of relief.

The black-shrouded thief threw down a ball on the ground and smoke exploded out, quickly filling the entire room.

Turnkey dropped to one knee and shot his weapon into the smoke, unleashing four electrified bursts into the room. The smoke turned blue as they passed through.

"Do you see her, Al?"

Al looked around and then started coughing from all the smoke in the room. "No. She's gone."

Turnkey muffled his mouth with his forearm to cover it from the smoke. He slowly and methodically moved toward Al but no attack came. The smoke began to dissipate and the agents found the room empty, except for the man knocked out on the floor. The thief and the Serpent's Blade were gone, and so were the answers.

Turnkey offered his hand to Al to help him up. "You all right, yo?"

"Yeah. Thanks for coming." Still coughing, Al asked, "Why are you dressed so nicely?"

Turnkey chuckled. "That's a long story, man. Come on, we don't have time to chit-chat. Do you know where she went? Is there another way out of this room?"

Al shook his head. "I don't know where she went, but I've got everything on audio." He turned off the watch recorder and ran a hand through his hair.

Turnkey motioned to the door. "Follow me. We need to get out of here before Heeto's men find us."

Al grabbed his backpack from the detention room. "Who's Heeto?"

"Oh, you know—one of the bad guys that keeps us employed."

~

Al and Turnkey navigated the tunnel system back to the arena level and exited.

Driving Turnkey's motorcycle, the two agents headed in the direction of the park to get Al's bike. On the way, Al told Turnkey about the exchange with the thief.

"Turnkey, if we send this audio file to Mary-Anne for analysis, she will find out about the email and the video. Then the Chief will find out too."

"Come on, man. We gotta trust the Chief with this. If this thief sent the email, then we have to let HQ know. Al, don't doubt them. Mary-Anne was trying earlier to tell you about the Dragon's Lair, but you cut her off. It's time to let them help us."

Al needed help. If the thief was telling the truth and didn't know about the video, why did she ask about his parents? More basic, how did she know his name, Dangermond?

Alabaster trusted his partner. "Fine, Turnkey, let's send it off to HQ and tell them about the email."

They arrived at the park and picked up Al's motorcycle right where they had left it. It was dark and no one was around. Al used his watch to make the video call to Headquarters.

"Oh, Al!" Mary-Anne said as she smiled at him. "Turnkey found you! Are you all right?

Al rubbed his cheek with his hand where he had been struck. "Sure thing, Mary-Anne, only a few scratches. Nothing permanent."

Mary-Anne spoke quickly. "We saw you come back on the VT just a while ago. We have you located in a park, but we couldn't get in touch with you once the VT found you."

Al nodded. "Yeah, I shut off the communication when I was in the Dragon's Lair. They had me hostage and I fought the thief who stole the blade, but she got away. I made a recording of the whole thing. Can you take a look and see if you can find any clues from it?"

Al looked over at Turnkey. "Oh, and Mary-Anne. I'm forwarding you an email I got a few days ago about my parents' murder."

Mary-Anne looked puzzled. "Their murder? Like an email about the car wreck?"

Al shook his head. "No. Just read the email. Then you'll understand."

The agent pressed a couple of buttons on his watch and the audio file was uploaded to Mary-Anne. Then he forwarded her the email with the attached video.

The girl looked to the side at her computer. "Okay, I have them. I will take a listen and let you know what I can find out. Here's Sensei Xu."

The bearded Chinese man appeared on the screen. "Agents, I am glad you are safe. Go to our Tokyo safe-house and make a formal report for this mission. We will discuss the details in the morning."

Turnkey grabbed Al's wrist so the martial arts master could see him. "Sensei Xu, I have recovered Tosaka Heeto's smart phone, which has his entire criminal network. What do you want me to do with it?"

The old sage raised his eyebrows. "Go to the Shinjuku and give it to Mr. Fudosan. He will know what to do with it. Anything else?"

Both agents had nothing more and they signed off. They drove to Fudosan's tower and told Sota of their failed attempt to recover the Serpent's Blade, but that HQ would provide a full report to Mr. Fudosan very soon. The agents handed the phone and the access code over to Sota. The Japanese man was deeply thankful—now Heeto would be exposed, and Mr. Fudosan would be pleased with this new development.

Al and Turnkey headed off on their motorcycles to the Universal Sports Academy campus near the outskirts of

Tokyo. Among the regular sports buildings was a secret and secure safe-house, similar to hundreds of others around the globe, for the undercover agents of the U.S.A.

Al was consumed with questions about the thief and his parents. He would stop at nothing to find the Serpent's Blade. Wherever it was, there was the thief. Wherever she was, so too was her boss, and the answers to the questions that burned inside him. He *had* to find her.

23

Life Debt

Dr. Zerick Moonshae examined the Serpent's Blade in the quiet of his enormous house. The large research room with red carpet had old oak tables all around. In his slick white suit, Moonshae stood in the center of the room with his treasure next to an old map. The sunlight from the windows reflected off the blade onto his brown hair and the thief noticed a slight tint of grey. How he could stand wearing that same white suit on his hot ocean island, she had no idea.

The clean-shaven man turned to her and smiled. "Ah, yes. Exquisite, is it not?"

"It's *great*... Does this resolve my debt to you?" the thief asked the boss.

"Oh, no. No...no, my dear, Katya, there are still many

more missions you must complete." He looked at his map. "And you will complete them all, with the same level of expertise… Unless, of course…," he turned to look at her, "you do not wish to see them again?"

The girl fidgeted, but then caught herself. She stood taller. "Yes sir. I will remain the Moon's Hand until I've satisfied the debt I owe you." She hated that. *What a stupid thing to call me*, she thought. It gave her even more reason to hate him.

He turned his attention back to the blade. "Good. Very good. And what of the sword knowledge—its history, eh?"

Katya looked at him. "Dangermond didn't learn anything from Fudosan. It looks like the Japanese man told him very little. I saw Alabaster's eyes and he was speaking the truth when I interrogated him."

The man raised his left eyebrow. "Alabaster?"

"Dangermond, I mean. Dangermond." She looked away to the floor. She already had said too much.

"Ah, so this Alabaster Dangermond got something from you, did he? Got you talking a little?"

Moonshae always saw through lies. She thought it was best to be honest, "Yes. He…he…offered me a job…if I would give up being a thief and return the sword. He—"

"Well, Katya, whatever he thinks he extracted from you, I am sure it is of no consequence. The U.S.A. has never known of my activities even though I know their most intimate plans. My operative is deep undercover inside their administration. It is laughable they would gain knowledge of me—how I orchestrate my will on the world.

They never will know me, until I choose to reveal myself to them. Is that clear?"

"Yes. Yes, sir. It is."

The well-dressed master turned back to the sword. "And what of the stone? Did he know anything about the stone his parents have hidden away?"

She shook her head. "He was very surprised by my inquiry. He accused me of sending an email."

"Good. Yes, very good. Perhaps now that I've planted the thought in his mind, this junior Dangermond will get curious and find what I seek. He will reveal its location and you will take it for me. It has taken me ten years since I first learned of it from his parents. I've secretly combed every inch of that Dangermond house, but I still haven't found it. I questioned his parents, but they were…less than helpful. I put them away, for good." The man clicked on a video screen for Katya to see.

The thief got the joke and she thought it was disgusting. Moonshae talked like he despised violence but his actions showed he cared nothing for other people's lives.

Moonshae clicked off the screen and looked at Katya. "I sent the young Dangermond a video of his parents in an email. Your question prompted him more. Now, he will surely find the stone for me. He's a clever boy. Since I couldn't find it, the only explanation is that his parents made it so only he could retrieve it. And when he does, it will be mine."

Katya felt sick to her stomach.

Moonshae examined the hilt of the sword. "The power

of this sword has been hidden for a thousand years. I will bring it to life, and then I will have my reward." He pointed the sword away from himself and moved one hand down the flat of the blade as he looked at it.

He quickly came out of his charmed trance and looked back at his map. "Cy is slowly making progress on the network, so I still have time to wait. You will find a half-million dollars have been deposited in your account, as normal. Go and tell Cy to send another shipment of plasma bullets to Heeto and equip them with new cars."

Moonshae leaned down near the map, his face just above Japan. "Did Heeto discover you stole the millions from him, or does he still think Dangermond stole the money in Thailand for Fudosan?"

The girl shook her head. "No, he thinks it was Dangermond, like you said I should say."

Moonshae raised an eyebrow. "Good. Then go to your home and wait there until I summon you."

The man looked up directly at her. "And Katya. I am always watching."

~

Katya returned to her home in Astana, the capital city of Kazakhstan, in the central heart of the Asian continent. Her residence was in the middle of the city within the Embassy District, near all the foreign embassies and the Palace. Katya lived on the top-most level of the Watergreen West residential building. It was a secluded and safe location she called home. She owned the entire top three floors of the tallest structure in the complex, considered an exclusive place to live.

Katya didn't trust Moonshae—she didn't trust anyone. Her home was full of the best security systems available. She specialized in breaking into everything and she had designed her own security measures.

Twelve floors up, her view was spectacular with windows from floor to ceiling, giving a panorama of the outside. All around she could see the skyscrapers of the city, including the Bayterek Tower, an observation tower similar to many of the structures in the greatest cities of the world. It reminded her of the Space Needle in Seattle. The Presidential Palace was just across the street in the most expensive part of the urban area. Although this apartment was not her original home, she did grow up in Astana.

The money Dr. Moonshae paid was enough for her to live in comfort like a queen and to have the best things to improve her craft, but she seethed in hatred of the man. He held her by a leash and she could not escape his hold on her. She didn't need reminding, but Alabaster Dangermond *had* reminded her of the pain—the aching hole in her heart.

She walked over to look out at the Emerald Towers complex, the tallest buildings in Astana. "No. I won't let that in," she said aloud to herself. She picked up the brush on the table and began to stroke her auburn hair.

The more she looked out the bedroom window, the angrier she felt. The cascade of heat rising up inside her was like water ready to boil. Moonshae had put her in this position and it was impossible. She *had* to work for him. She *had* to finish the missions. She had to keep doing his bidding. She owed it to them. She would do anything for them. She loved them.

She took her brush and threw it across the room, shattering a vase full of fresh flowers. The brush fell to the floor alongside the shattered bits of glass and the bouquet. Katya fell down to her knees and began to weep next to the window.

From a clandestine room in the next building over, Al asked Turnkey, "What did she just throw?"

24

In the Hard Place

"I think it was her hair brush."

Al looked at a monitor. "Looks like she's pretty upset. Infrared shows she's crying." He zoomed in with the digital camera and confirmed she was definitely crying.

The two agents stood in the northern Emerald Tower across from the Watergreen West residential building, peering into the windows of the thief's home. It had taken them four days, but the U.S.A. had found this elusive thief.

Before leaving Japan, the guys gave HQ a briefing report about all that happened. Al inquired with the Chief about the stone, but the large man didn't know anything. The Chief and Sensei Xu were in agreement that the guys should come home, but Al begged the Chief to allow them to continue the investigation. Turnkey said it would give them more experience in real training. In the end, the Chief decided to allow them to continue the investigation because of the possible connection with Al's parents and because of the skill both agents showed in the field, but the two dispatched senior agents were going to go with them as backup.

Given time to rest and recover, the guys went off to climb some of the rock faces of Japanese mountains while they waited on the analysis of the Dragon's Lair conversation. Climbing gave Al and Turnkey time to think about the video of his parents. It also gave them time to talk. In the early evening of the second day in Japan, it was Mary-Anne who alerted them to look for the thief in Astana.

Mary-Anne was a genius. From the audio conversation Al had with the thief in the dungeons of the Dragon's Lair, she analyzed the ever-so-slight accent of the thief's voice. The thief's spoken English and her tones and rhythms of the English language were the same sounds from northern Indiana, a Midwestern state in the United States of America, where American-English accent is minimal by native speakers. But for Mary-Anne, through her advanced acoustic analysis technology, the words of the thief rang out loud and clear that she was from Kazakhstan, and specifically from Astana. Al thought it amazing how the sound of one's voice could be clearly linked to geography.

Once the U.S.A. had narrowed down the place they were looking for, it was only a matter of time to stake out the central city residential locations where a high-profile thief might live. After all, most thieves enjoyed the spoils of their stolen goods and that usually put them in the most expensive part of town. The two senior agents dispatched with them stayed in the Astana field office, in case they were needed. Sensei Xu argued that if Al and Turnkey remained in the field, they should proceed without the senior agents as much as possible as part of their training. The Chief agreed.

They had a visual on the thief, but no audio. Al wondered why she was crying. He hadn't cried like that since…since the time he dropped to his knees when he saw his parents murdered in the video. Al really missed them. And now he had found the girl with the Serpent's Blade, who had asked about his parents. It was time to find out what she knew about them and get that sword back.

~

Katya stared to the side, as if in a daze.

She would give up her life as a thief if she had the choice. Yes, her missions had brought her money and, except for the one job in which she was caught stealing three years ago, her sneaky ways and strength had been perfect. She had accumulated precious treasures under Moonshae's thumb, but she would give it all up if only…

"My dears, my precious ones…" After a minute of staring at the floor, she shook out of her trauma.

"No…no," she said calmly, regaining her composure. "I will save you. I will save you both and I will get Moonshae all the treasures he wants. Then, in the moment when I'm with you, I will defeat him once and for all and we will escape…never to be seen again."

Katya got up and wiped the tears from her face. She looked out at the buildings, feeling the warmth of the sunshine blazing in through the glass window. She felt better and she began to think clearly.

No one would stand in her way. She would not let anyone prevent her from stealing what Dr. Zerick Moonshae wanted. Katya wouldn't resort to her boss's lethality, but if it came down to Alabaster Dangermond or them, she would choose them. She would do anything to save her precious sisters.

Katya moved away from the west windows and checked the messages on her phone—nothing from Dr. Moonshae yet. When would he call? She cleaned up the broken glass and put her brush back in its place, but she was restless. Waiting around was driving her crazy, so she tried occupying herself with some music. That didn't help get her sisters out of her head. She tried watching TV, but that didn't help either. The book picked up off the coffee table was put back down right away. She groaned.

She always came and went as she pleased, so to clear her mind she decided to go out. Katya grabbed her sunglasses and phone and headed in her private elevator down to her garage in the basement of the complex. As the elevator doors opened in the garage, she had plenty of cars to choose from. Dr. Z's money had paid for all of them, none of which were less than $100,000. At fifteen years old, her money let her do whatever she wanted in Astana. She held numerous fake

IDs, including one that said she was eighteen—the legal age to drive in Kazakhstan. Looking around at the display of powerful vehicles, she chose the red Lamborghini with winged doors that opened skyward instead of away from the car. She wanted to go fast, and the Lamborghini would do 200 miles per hour easily on the desert steppe roads of rural Kazakhstan.

Pressing the ignition button, the engine roared to life. *This will do.*

"Welcome," the car said, "What would you like to do?"

She grasped the steering wheel. "I'm in charge today. Set for manual driving." The car acknowledged manual driving and turned complete control over to Katya. Heading up an incline to the main street, a huge metal door rose and off she went onto the boulevard.

~

They had seen the thief get into the elevator and head down. Now, seeing the red sports car emerge from the lower levels onto the street prompted Al and Turnkey to focus on the road.

Al looked out the window. "Whoa. Do you see that? Is that her in that car?"

Turnkey zoomed the camera onto the darkened car windshield. "Hang on…switching to infrared," he said, pressing a couple of buttons on the keyboard connected to the high-resolution camera.

Turnkey nodded. "Yep, that's her. I think this is our chance, yo."

Al looked at Turnkey. "Okay. Let's go break into that place and see if we can find the Serpent's Blade or figure out who she is working for." *And maybe I can get some answers about my parents.*

25

Flying Escapades

The two agents went to the top of the Emerald Tower. It stood nearly 500 feet tall and the fierce wind buffeted it from all directions.

Turnkey and Al decided that the only way they could get into the thief's home was from the roof of her complex. The Emerald Tower was the closest building next to the complex, only separated by a parking lot, and was the only structure nearby that was taller. The thief's roof was over 400 feet away from the top of the Emerald Tower when the agents digitally measured it with their distance-sight.

"No way…" Al said under his breath.

Pulling out the Kevlar strength cord, the guys confirmed it was not going to be nearly long enough—they only had 220 feet of rope.

Al shrugged his shoulders. "Well, I was really hoping we could zip line across to the roof. That would have been so sport'n."

Turnkey looked in different directions. "Yeah, me too. We'll have to find another way."

The wind howled on the roof as the agents discussed a different entry. Turnkey pointed to the thief's building. "That exterior looks slow to climb and probably has sensors that will set off alarms, so we can't go that way."

"See there." He pointed to a row of architectural circles on the building just below the thief's floor. "That looks like part of the structure, but I bet it has sensors that would detect a climber and lock down her whole place."

As they stood there looking and swaying from the gusts of the wind on the roof, they surveyed the whole complex. There weren't many options. Looking down, Al saw an assortment of cars and motorcycles stopping and going on the street. And then it hit him.

Al jumped and pointed. "Motorcycles!"

"What?" his friend said, trying to find the same location Al was looking at on the street.

Alabaster turned to his partner. "Motorcycles. We can use our motorcycles to get us onto that roof!"

"How? What do you mean, yo?"

"In Tokyo, Mary-Anne said our motorcycles have turbo-lifters. They can boost us up to that roof. What were those specs, again?"

Turnkey remembered, "It was 130 miles per hour for a 130-foot launch."

"1, 2….8…12, 13 stories. Well, there we go. That building roof is 130 feet tall…give or take a couple of feet. We can do it." Al smiled.

Turnkey frowned. "Give or take a couple of feet? We? Maybe *you* can, but look, Al, that's crazy—totally loco, man. You can't do that. If you fail, the Chief would—"

"Come on, Turnkey. It's our only play."

The taller teen agent shook his head. "That's just crazy, man." Turnkey used a digital distance sight to measure the building to see if Al was right. It was 128 feet tall. "Okay, man. You're crazy, but I'll monitor you from here."

He shook his head again. "What are you going to do if the motorcycle can't get you high enough?"

Al laughed. "Umm…yeah. I guess I'll figure it out."

∼

On his motorcycle, Al drove away from the thief's building to get as much distance to build up speed as possible. With the busy street traffic, the best approach was to drive from the Emerald Tower toward the thief's building on the empty pedestrian sidewalk, into the parking lot between the buildings and then launch to the roof. The hedges and trees throughout the nearly empty parking lot would provide enough cover that the launch wouldn't be seen by anyone, unless they were looking right at the thief's building.

Turnkey stayed on the roof to monitor the op. They went communication silent until Alabaster was on the roof of the thief's building.

In order to get maximum height, the motorcycle would need to achieve a speed of at least 130 miles per hour. The jump could be achieved given the distance from Al's current position to the launch point according to the onboard computer, but the angle from the launch had to be perfect.

If Al deviated even slightly, the turbo-lift wouldn't be enough to clear the edge wall around the roof. Even though the motorcycle had an autopilot, the turbo-lifters would not engage in that mode, for safety reasons. That meant Al would have to drive it fast to the launch point and hope for the best to achieve the correct angle. He decided to use the motorcycle auto-pilot for as long as possible and try to get the bike to drive anyway.

"Okay Bike, autopilot to launch point at 135 miles per hour for an optimum launch angle." He wanted the extra five miles per hour more to make sure the turbo lifters engaged.

The bike responded, "Turbo-lifters will not engage in auto-pilot. You will be required to manually drive from position X." A red X appeared on the helmet display.

"Okay Bike, can you autopilot up to that point and give manual control once reaching that X-point, and then engage turbo-lifters on my mark?"

"Yes. Is that what you desire?" the computer asked.

"Yes."

Adrenaline coursed through his veins. "Okay Bike. Engage that action on my mark. Three…two…one… Mark!"

The back wheel spun with immense rotation, leaving a skid mark on the pavement, and exploded forward with tremendous power, popping a small wheelie.

It was a good thing the bike was in autopilot because the sidewalk was uneven and there were cracks in the parking lot. Al bumped and thrust around with the rapid acceleration.

The black motorcycle pierced the air with aerodynamic velocity—90 mph...100 mph...110 mph...120 mph...130 mph...

Al reached the point of manual override much quicker than he anticipated. The motorcycle was traveling 135 miles per hour when Al took over. The handle grips were shaking with turbulence from the uneven parking lot. He hit the launch point.

"Mark!"

Alabaster Dangermond's motorcycle launched into the air from the parking lot with maximum velocity. The front wheel launcher went first, forcing a wheelie and an explosion of fire rocketed out of the back of the motorcycle. Al held on for dear life, hoping the angle was right as the machine flew through the air.

The motorcycle approached the roof wall of the building within a few seconds and the display sensor in Al's helmet began warning alarms.

"Danger! Danger! Clearance threshold not achieved. Impact imminent!" said the digital onboard computer voice.

He wasn't going to make it. He was going to crash into the wall.

Alabaster pulled hard on his handle grips to get his feet under him. Stepping on the seat cushion, he braced himself as quickly as he could to jump up in the air just before his motorcycle hit the building. The empty space was disappearing at a rate quicker than he could adapt. Seeing the wall approach in a blur, Alabaster jumped with all the strength he could muster into the air and launched himself off of the motorcycle, 130 feet off the ground.

26

Record Book

The rocketing black motorcycle slammed hard into the green-shaded exterior roof wall—the bike didn't make it. As it disappeared beneath him, plummeting toward the ground, the agent soared over the wall with arms flailing and legs in motion, as if in a run. Al tried to tuck into a roll with the roof floor coming fast. At 135 miles per hour, human bodies were not designed to come to an immediate stop and he hoped his plan would work. Otherwise, he was dead.

He expected his speed and nearness to the rooftop would initiate the Impact Suit, but it did not. Hoping to hear the suit engage, only silent wind rushed into his ears. He hit the roof in a vicious somersault roll. It was a good thing his helmet was so perfectly conformed to his head because he took more than a few blows that would have killed him on the spot.

As he tumbled, the friction of the roof surface gripped his outer clothing, ripping it to shreds. If it weren't for his Kevlar-strength body armor underneath, he would have been skinned alive from the rough roof surface. As he approached the opposite wall at the end of the roof, the Impact Suit partially engaged where the suit wasn't ripped. Half-protected, he hit the wall with a hard thud that knocked the wind out of his lungs and then bounced him away from the wall. The late expansion of the suit saved every bone in his upper body from being snapped into a hundred pieces.

Al gasped for air, but none could be found. His helmet was wrapped in plastic and the small space between his mouth and the glass of his helmet was inadequate to give him back breath from the colossal crash. Alabaster Dangermond began to suffocate.

Al tried to move but his arms were trapped by the Impact Suit. With no air he disappeared into the blackness...

~

He dreamt he was skydiving, soaring like an eagle against the wind as he fell to Earth.

"—l!"

"Al!"

"Al! Wake up! Al, come in! Al! Come in!"

Am I dead?

Turnkey?

Al wheezed out his partner's name, "Turnkey."

"Al! Hey, man, are you all right?"

Where am I? The thoughts swirled in his head as the

aches in his body caused him to cringe in pain. *What happened?*

Alabaster Dangermond felt like he had just gone through a washing machine and ultra-fast dry cycle. Tumbled and dazed, he breathed hard, still gasping for air even though the Impact Suit had disengaged. He fell back into a dream stupor and lost consciousness.

~

Al felt the warmth from the sun on his face. It was safe and comforting. He was at the beach his parents used to take him to in Newport, Rhode Island, when he was little. Both his parents were there with him and he wanted to stay there forever. Then he heard his friend. Turnkey doesn't belong here...

Turnkey yelled again. "Come on, yo, say something! Al, are you all right?"

Al moaned.

"Arrr...okay... Okay, Turnkey. Pipe down. I...I can hear you." It took most of his strength to speak.

Turnkey spoke quickly. "Oh man, Al. You all right?"

Al moved his arms slowly and propped himself up. "Yeah, I think so." He tried to stand but sat back down immediately. He sighed. As he slumped, he focused on the tower skyscraper in the distance and waited for the dizzy feelings to subside.

"I wasn't sure you were going to make it, homie!"

"Me, either. Me, either... uh... That was stupid," Al said. "But, that must've looked pretty sport'n," he added quietly.

Turnkey laughed. "Well…yeah…that was off the hook. You're crazy, man. Crazy. That was one for the record books, Al."

Al crawled over to the wall and slumped on it for support. "That's one record I could have done without." Then he pushed himself up and puked over the roof edge onto someone's balcony below. That made him feel a lot better but he felt bad for the resident who would find the disgusting present on their balcony. Maybe if it rained it would wash the mess away before it was found.

"Don't be crazy like that again," Turnkey said. "And maybe that's one detail we'll leave out of our report to the Chief." Al was surprised by his partner's words. Turnkey never omitted anything, but Al wasn't going to argue with his friend.

Resting for a few minutes, Al put his head in an upright position and set it against the wall as he assessed the damage to his body. When he took off the Impact Suit and the Kevlar body protection pieces, surprisingly he only had bruises on his forearms to accompany some on his thighs. His chest felt like a vise had crushed it, but nothing felt broken.

"Can you stand?" Turnkey asked.

"I think so," Al said as he slowly pulled himself up to a standing position.

Bracing himself on the wall, he spit until his mouth felt a little better from the vomit taste. But his esophagus still burned a little. "That was quite a ride. I thought the Impact Suit was going to engage. I guess it doesn't work unless you are falling down. Better talk to Mary-Anne about it."

As he stood there, he still felt a little dizzy. "What about the bike?" Al hoped his motorcycle wasn't destroyed.

Turnkey chuckled. "That thing? Oh, man, when it hit the wall it fell like a meteor from space and slammed into the bushes next to the parking lot. From what I can tell, it's concealed behind the foliage."

Al laughed quietly, even though it hurt. "She sure knows how to build 'em, doesn't she?"

"Hey, Al, it looks like we've got some visitors. All the trees between the parking lot and the street shielded your ride, but some residents are coming out of the building. Hold your position and don't look over the wall," Turnkey said. "There are about a dozen people looking around—they probably heard the loud bang against the building."

Al sat back down and took out two granola bars from his pocket to boost his energy as he waited. The pause gave Al the time he needed to regain his composure.

After a few minutes, Turnkey came back on the comm channel. "Okay, yo. They didn't find your motorcycle. Looks like the coast is clear, when you're ready."

Al stretched and took off his small waist pack. From inside it, he pulled out the black Chameleon Pannus suit. He put it on slowly and checked the Amber Alchemy power pack to verify it wasn't damaged. If the electro-chemical power supply was damaged, the suit would fail to make the wearer invisible for thirty minutes after activation.

"Proceeding to stage two," Al said.

He stuffed the remains of the Impact Suit into his helmet, and hid the helmet and the pieces of the Kevlar body armor behind some roofing machinery, just in case somebody came looking on the roof for the source of the loud crash. He affixed a communication earpiece into his left ear so he could talk directly to Turnkey and still be hands-free.

Alabaster Dangermond moved over to an access roof port and opened it. It was unlocked. The agent entered the port and moved into the duct system of the residential building. He was concealed in black from head to toe—he had not turned on the invisibility suit, yet.

"Good luck, yo, and be careful—that thief girl might have traps for uninvited guests," Turnkey said.

"I'm ready for anything." Al still ached all over and wondered if he really was ready for anything. He would soon find out.

27

Death Trap

Looking everywhere for sensor traps, Al crawled on his hands and knees through the large air duct from the roof. His legs felt like they had extra 40lb weights on them from the motorcycle stunt on the roof. He swore he would never do something that crazy again.

He came to a junction and entered the main system of the building. The air duct was a maze of many large and small metal passages behind the walls and in the ceilings of all the rooms in the building. Alabaster saw a chart at the junction that included a map of the nearby section of ducts. It was written in Russian, but he was able to make out where each of the ducts led from the map. Al could read a couple of languages, but not Russian. His foreign language speaking skills were less than desirable—he was only fluent in French and that was because he was strong in his Latin studies—a requirement for all secret agents.

Al's concealed earpiece let him communicate directly with Turnkey. "TK. I have a beat on the thief's apartment."

"Roger that."

Al turned down the last passage toward the thief's home and saw an immediate problem. "Oh, man, that's not cool."

"What's not cool?"

Al was almost above the thief's apartment in the duct. "She has a laser beam system protecting the air duct access. I'm going to have to bypass it somehow."

Turnkey started typing on his computer and Al could hear him through the comm channel. "If you disturb any of the lasers, it'll probably trigger the alarm system."

Al didn't have any gadgets on him other than his watch. "Okay, bro, I have an idea. Stand-by."

He moved toward the laser-protected panel. The panel was a large ceiling grate for airflow and Al could partially see through it down into the thief's large bedroom. The panel looked flush with the ceiling and about 6 inches above the panel was the laser system, shooting out a continuous red beam that bounced all around on mirrors. Moving the grate was impossible with the laser beams in the way.

Al saw a key pad on the duct wall. It had to be the controls for the laser but no external port was visible to by-pass the code, so he focused on the grate laser array.

Pulling up his sleeve, Al aimed his watch laser at the grate beam emitter to burn it out. He pushed the button and ignited his watch laser. He held it for at least thirty seconds, but nothing happened.

"Any ideas about what I can do?" Al asked. "My watch laser didn't have any effect on the beam emitter."

"Do you have any mirrors, yo? You could use them to deflect the beam back on itself and move the grate."

Al shook his head. "No, man, I don't have any mirrors. And by the time you delivered them over here, she would be back. But, I'm not giving up." Alabaster turned his attention to the keypad. "Oh, man, no way."

"What?"

"The laser is off," Al laughed.

"Say what?"

Al laughed even harder. "Check it out, man. The guys who installed this laser system must have thought no one would ever be trying to break in through the duct. They etched the code for the laser shutdown right into the metal on the duct wall next to the keypad." Turnkey laughed too.

Al unlocked the panel and let the grate swing open into the thief's bedroom. He lowered himself down into the room and stepped onto the large bed.

Turnkey spoke first. "Hey, yo, I see you."

Al waved out the window from the bed.

"Nice, Al. Now quit messing around and get to work."

Before stepping off the bed, Alabaster peered toward the floorboards, looking for hidden laser ports. He saw none and stepped down. If she had an alarm system, the most likely place for controls was next to the front door—the elevator in the next room.

The thief kept a tidy home. Her minimal possessions looked expensive. Al searched for clues to her identity but found nothing. The thief had no photos in the apartment. Content with his examination of the room, he made his way out into the living quarters and the kitchen, moving cautiously with each step.

The expansive living area had tall windows and a kitchen to the side. Furniture dotted the sparse room. Expensive artwork hung on the walls, the kind only found in museums by the master artists of the past. Across the room was the elevator door, but there was no security panel to been seen.

"This feels too easy, Turnkey. Why would she leave and not have a security system? There are thousands of dollars in paintings on these walls."

"Al, I can see your every move. Be careful."

The agent continued his investigation and stayed alert, but the slower and more cautious he moved, the more his body hurt. He swung his arms to stretch them, trying to stay loose. "Moving toward the kitchen."

A flooring change marked the boundary into the kitchen with a transition from wood to tile. The kitchen was huge. In the center was a large kitchen island with a black granite countertop. Inlaid into the center of the granite was a large jade mineral. Pots and pans that looked like they'd never been used before hung from the ceiling. Just before stepping onto the kitchen tile, Al paused.

In line with the boundary of the kitchen tile, on the wall, he saw a series of vertical holes. The holes went from floor to ceiling with a new hole about every six inches. On the opposite wall was the same pattern, offset by a few inches. *Is this some kind of laser beam security system?*

Reaching in through a pocket slit in the invisibility suit, he took some climbing chalk powder from a small bag on his belt and tossed it in the air across the threshold to see if he could see a beam. Nothing.

"TK, do you see anything with the spectral viewer? Any beams in this area?"

Al heard Turnkey type something on his keyboard. "Nothing, man. But I might be too far out or the outer glass might be shielded somehow."

The agent positioned his feet in an athletic stance and did a karate-chop through the air with his hand. Pin darts shot through the air from both directions along the threshold and stuck into the wood. Al's hand was too quick for the darts. Before he could investigate them, he heard a noise like a motor crank.

Around the apartment home, a series of cages began to descend from the ceiling. Masked ceiling panels opened and iron bars slammed down to the floor forming a maze in the room. The first set covered the windows, walls, and the paintings. The next set formed section barriers around the furniture. A panel opened above him. Al had no choice. He karate chopped hard to set off as many darts as he could and then dove into the kitchen as a set of bars dropped from the ceiling, nearly missing him where he had just stood. Thankfully, no more darts shot out of the holes when he plunged forward.

Turnkey yelled. "Yo!"

Al rolled onto the tile and popped right up.

"Security system activated, Turnkey."

The tile in the kitchen began to heat up and change color. A powerful roar from the kitchen vent sounded, creating a suction vacuum pulling the air out of the apartment. Pressure immediately built in Al's ear, making his eardrums feel like exploding.

"The tile is melting my boots, bro—I can't get out of this area!"

The floor tiles were now red from heat.

Turnkey shouted at him, "Get up on something!"

Jumping up onto the island, Al stood up and looked around, searching for a plan of action. Thinking the computer screen next to the cabinets across the tile might shut down the system, he prepared to make a jump to the other countertop along the wall. As he readied, he looked down. His boots wouldn't move. The melted rubber of his soles had stuck to the cool granite countertop—his footwear was useless. His boots smelled like burnt rubber.

"Well, there goes my element of surprise. That thief surely is on her way back now," he yelled to his partner above the noise of the venting system.

"Can you get out of there, Al?"

"No way, man, I'm stuck."

"Ah, man, come on, you've got to be kidding me," Turnkey said. "That thief is back in her red car. She must've already been on the way back. She's pulling into the garage right now."

28

Earful Approach

Al stepped out of his boots and jumped across the wave of heat shooting from the tile floor to the other countertop along the wall. He pushed on the touch screen. A bunch of words in Russian appeared, but then a barely audible female voice with a British accent asked, "How may I help you?"

The air was getting thinner as it was being sucked out.

He yelled above the roar of the suction venting. "Reset all security systems!"

"Passphrase, please."

"Ah, geesh. Come on." Al looked at the elevator, but there was no activity or lights. He knew she was going to show up any second.

"Incorrect. Passphrase, please."

Al didn't have a passphrase and he didn't know the thief well enough to guess what she would have set as the password.

The computer repeated the request. "Passphrase, please."

Al yelled out his best guess. "The Serpent's Blade."

"Incorrect. One last try before lockdown." Al hit the red button on the touchscreen and shut down the computer.

"Any help, TK?" His partner was a whiz at hacking into computer systems.

"Already on it, yo! Hang on…" Turnkey said.

"Come on, Turnkey," Al yelled, looking over to the elevator. Now a single activation light next to the elevator was on—the thief was coming up the shaft.

Al pulled the mask over his head and pressed the buttons on his suit. He disappeared under a blanket of invisibility. Without boots on, he would be virtually silent if he moved.

Al whispered so quietly, he could hardly hear himself, "Come on, Turnkey."

It was too late. The elevator arrived with a ding. The doors opened and the thief peeked out with her guns pointing forward. Air from the elevator rushed into the room, blowing her hair everywhere. Al froze on the countertop.

She yelled through the caged bars that were in front of the elevator, blocking her entry. "Who's in here?"

Turnkey spoke in a soft whisper into Al's earpiece. "I got it, man."

The security system began to shut down. Al noticed he was breathing hard from lack of air and quickly calmed himself with deep breaths through his nose.

The tiles stopped heating and reversed color. The iron bars ascended into the ceiling. The venting fan slowed in the kitchen and turned off completely. The home was essentially back to normal. Except for one thing—Al's boots were still stuck to the granite countertop. The lingering scent of burnt rubber wafted through the air.

The thief moved cautiously out of the elevator toward the kitchen with guns drawn. She looked at the darts in the wall and the boots attached to the island countertop. Seeing no one, the thief turned and stepped toward the living areas in the direction of the paintings on the wall.

Invisible, Al crouched right next to her on the countertop.

The thief shouted loudly. "Show yourself!"

There was only silence.

As she systematically moved through the apartment, Al could hear her speak. "When I catch you, things will be over for you, friend." Al wanted to move, but decided to stay put.

The thief moved back into the kitchen to access the touch screen computer next to Al. She was inches away from him. He tried to move away from her without notice, but Al saw his gig was up when she flinched and looked in his direction when he moved.

The thief turned to raise her guns right up at him as he kicked hard, knocking the guns out of her hands. She lost her balance and fell backward, hitting the granite kitchen island.

She recovered quickly.

Al jumped off the countertop as she tried to ram him off it. She caught his leg and he came crashing down onto the tile and let out a groan. Another bruise to add to his collection.

Hearing his sound she drop-kicked right at his head.

Running on pure adrenaline, Al rolled away from the hit as she began to stomp on the ground with her powerful legs.

She tumbled to the ground as Al grabbed ahold of her foot and twisted it to the side.

She groaned, hitting her hands down on the wood planks in apparent disgust as she got up. "You're a dead man."

With fists clenched ready to attack, she closed her eyes.

Was she seriously going to fight him even though he was invisible? *She's good, but not that good.*

She launched an attack. Swinging with all limbs in a cartwheel, she moved forward connecting a blow to Al's shoulder. She kicked and slammed into his stomach. Al hit the floor hard and let out a loud moan.

"Gotcha!" she said in triumph.

Her fist came down onto his cheek at the same moment he kicked up, sending her sprawling to the side, off-balance. Gaining a foothold, she charged him with reckless abandon. He couldn't get out of the way and she connected with his torso as she ran into him. Al dropped down to the ground and moved to the side. She turned and charged again and he tripped her ankle. The thief stumbled forward and crashed into the bedroom door, smacking her head hard on the wood. She tried to get up and fell backward into the bedroom. Al got up, ready for another attack, but the thief lay motionless on the ground. Al moved cautiously over to her and checked her pulse. It was strong.

"She's knocked out, TK."

Turnkey let out a sigh. "That was crazy. I can't believe she actually tried to fight you."

"I know."

Al looked down at her and felt new respect and admiration for her.

Turnkey spoke. "Al, yo. We've got action on the roof. A sweet chopper with full weaponry just landed on the helipad on top of Watergreen East. They're probably her back-up. Those guys are packing heavy weapons. Hurry up."

Al checked her again and then left the bedroom to go back to the computer display in the kitchen. "Hey, man, do you still have access to the computer?"

"Yo, I totally hacked it with a syllable reconstruction of that thief's voice. I bypassed the low-grade encryption for the three passphrase limit and applied the file Mary-Anne gave me of the thief's voice until I got the passphrase to shut down the security. Voice passphrase is, 'Three fair maidens'."

Al got into the computer with *three fair maidens* and began a search.

"Computer, show me all files on the Serpent's Blade."

"There are no files with those search key words," the computer replied.

"Computer, show me all files on Viking King Olaf Tryggvason."

Turnkey jumped in. "Yo, Al. I already tried those. She doesn't have anything on the sword. Hurry it up, you're running out of time."

"Maybe she has personal logs? Computer, show me personal logs by…," he still didn't know this thief's name. "Show me all personal logs."

"Personal log access passphrase, please."

Al threw his hands up. "Oh, man, come on!"

At that moment the elevator dinged, and the doors opened into the apartment home.

29

Black Web

"Oh, Katya! Dear Katya…are you here?" called out the man dressed in a fine white suit. He walked with a cane but strolled through the room with carefree steps. His three bodyguards spread throughout the room, packing heavy, large guns.

He called out again. "Oh, Katya! Are you home?"

Katya—so that's her name.

Invisible, Alabaster heard from behind, "Personal log access passphrase please." It was the computer talking to him.

The finely-dressed man looked over, his eyes piercing the space directly where Alabaster stood in front of the computer. The man with the cane stood motionless and stared for a good ten seconds…

"Curious." His eyes remained fixed on Al's spot for a long moment, before shifting his gaze to the side, where the boots were stuck to the granite.

He looked over to one of his bodyguards. "Boggs."

"Sir?"

"You and Choy check the apartment."

"Yes, sir." The bodyguard motioned to the nearest man to begin searching the place.

"And you, Yuri, stand right there next to that kitchen island," the man said, pointing to a spot that would block Alabaster's exit into the living area from the kitchen. The guard moved over, his huge frame restricting the area.

Can he see me? Al moved slowly and quietly to his right. His joints felt stiff as he moved.

Boggs yelled from the bedroom. "Sir! Katya is in here. She's unconscious. There's a grate open into the vents!"

"Secure the room, Boggs." The well-dressed man began unscrewing the pommel on his cane top—a white knob with ornate swirled carvings in an unrecognizable pattern.

The man called out to everyone in the apartment home. "Stand-by, men, and prepare for Nightshade." He twisted the top of his cane and waited about 20 seconds. During the pause, he and his men put on goggles.

He double-tapped his cane to the ground, and the room went completely black!

Turnkey gasped. "Al. What happened? The whole room just went pitch black."

Unlike the night, with a moon to give light, this darkness was thick like black tar. Alabaster looked to the sides but could not see anything in the room. The living area disappeared into inky blackness. The countertops next to him were gone. The floor and ceiling were nothing but a wall of dark. Al waved his arm in the air but remembered he was invisible—he couldn't see his hand anyway. In a split second, a flash of light appeared and Alabaster felt a sensation he never experienced before.

Falling to the ground, Al writhed in horrid pain. The electric shock coursing through him set his blood on fire. He shouted out as the stick burned its electrifying power into him. As he shook uncontrollably in pain on the floor, the light stopped. It was all over.

Alabaster Dangermond could smell his own singed hair. His taught body stayed stiff and he felt as if every joint was locked. He heard a double-tap from the cane and sunlight turned on like a flashlight, pouring in from the window and blinding him. He shut his eyes.

"Ah, what do we have here?" the well-dressed man said, standing over him. Al looked up with squinted eyes but still couldn't see from the intense sunlight.

"Yuri, secure him," the boss said. Alabaster's blanket of invisibility was gone. Mary-Anne's suit could not handle the electrical shock.

The man in the white suit pointed to one of the sofas in the living area. "Set him over there."

～

Turnkey saw everything once the blackness was gone. "Al! Al! Can you hear me?" Turnkey shouted into the mic again and again. All he heard was empty silence. Communication channels had been cut. Turnkey was no longer in contact with his partner.

Watching the apartment home from the Emerald Tower, Turnkey saw the well-dressed man move toward the bedroom and disappear. The blinds on all the windows began to shut, and with them, his friend disappeared from sight too. Turnkey abandoned the observation post and prepared to rescue Al.

30

Moonbeams

The well-dressed man motioned to Boggs. "Move her into the living area, next to this one." The burly man complied, lifting the thief up into his arms as he carried her into the living area. He laid her down on a sofa near Alabaster.

Al's hands were bound and he was secured on the couch. Even if he wanted to escape, the bones in his body ached from the electrical shock—he wasn't going anywhere. He felt like sleeping for a week.

"Now, who do we have here, hmm?" the man said, as he motioned to Yuri to take off Al's mask. The bodyguard obeyed and removed the invisibility suit mask.

"Ah! You must be Mr. Dangermond! Katya has told me all about you and all that blade business." The man bowed slightly toward Alabaster. "What a pleasant surprise. So good of you to join us today and what a pleasure to make your acquaintance. Please accept my humble apologies for that rather nasty little business with my Electro-cane."

Al looked at the man and spoke in a raspy voice. "Who are you?" He felt more exhausted than he ever had.

"Ah, yes, but of course. Let me be so kind as to introduce myself. I am Dr. Zerick Moonshae." The well-dressed man smiled and looked at Al with piercing green eyes.

Al looked over at Katya.

Moonshae nodded. "It would appear you two must have had a little run-in."

"Yeah, well…"

Moonshae turned to one of his bodyguards and extended his hand. "Choy." The large guard handed the boss one of Katya's touch-screen tablets.

"Ah, it is right here, Mr. Dangermond! See." The man replayed the fight between Al and Katya, recorded by the hidden cameras throughout the apartment. The replay began from the moment when the darts were triggered. Al watched the security measures unfold and how Katya fought an invisible man on the screen.

"Very impressive. Very impressive, indeed!" Moonshae's voice cracked. "That must be the work of someone very special to have made an invisibility suit like that! Where might I find such a person?"

Al stared at him with his lips sealed.

"You might have made a fool of me, too, with your hidden ways. Shame on you for hiding in such a manner, Mr. Dangermond!"

Al struggled as he nodded toward the cane. "I see you've got your little gadgets, too," he whispered.

Bending down near to Alabaster's ear, he spoke quietly, "Ah…yes. Yes, I do. So much more than you know, boy."

Al just wanted to sleep. He had no more strength to fight. He glanced downward toward his bound hands and looked back up. His watch was under the sleeve, but he couldn't access it to cut the bindings. He wasn't sure it was even working after that electric shock.

"Tell me, Mr. Dangermond, what was it you sought from dear Katya? Why the sneaking around?"

"You know what I was looking for. She has the Serpent's Blade. The sword she stole. I want it back."

Moonshae began to pace back and forth slowly. "And what of it, hmm? Why do you seek such a treasure? Oh yes, that's right. Katya told me you tried to stop her from acquiring it in Tokyo. She said you were hired by the owner."

Al glared at Moonshae. "Who are you?"

"Me? Come now, Mr. Dangermond, must you be so naïve? Surely, you've figured it out. I'm the one who hired her for the job. I'm her boss."

He sent the email.

Al leaned forward and shouted as loud as he could muster, "Why did you kill my parents?" He collapsed backward with no strength left.

"Yes. Yes, my boy. I sent the email. And yes, I sent Katya to retrieve the sword. Such a nice ancient blade. I am very happy to give it back to you, once I am done with it. But first, before I return the sword to you, I will need you, of course, to join me on a little journey. A journey…yes…that will allow you to be reunited with the Serpent's Blade."

"Prepare the copter," the boss said to Boggs, who relayed the message to the roof.

Moonshae motioned to Yuri and the thug pulled out a needle.

"And now, Mr. Dangermond, I hope you will permit me the honor of joining me on a delicious journey—"

Al shook his head. "No, stop." The needle went right into his neck.

"…a delicious journey…"

Alabaster's vision went dark as he slipped away into the void.

31

Lost

Turnkey scaled the Watergreen East residential building, trying to reach the helipad on the roof. Using a series of ropes and suctions, he scaled it without any notice from inside or out.

On a ledge, he peeked over the short wall on the roof. Two well-armed men were standing guard. A third guard walked slowly around the helicopter. They held semi-automatic guns, but Turnkey could not identify them. Inside the large, well-armed helicopter sat the pilot, who had started it again—this bird was about to fly off.

He pressed his watch to contact the local senior agents that had come to Astana with them. He activated the homing beacon on his watch and left them a brief recorded message requesting backup.

Taking another peek, he waited until the roaming guard was out of line-of-sight and pulled out a mini-camera and put it on top of the wall. It was small and discrete, unlikely to attract attention. Staying on the exterior ledge, out of sight, he used a small hand-held device the size of a smartphone to control the camera. He snapped a couple of shots of the crescent moon insignia on the side of the copter. Maybe Mary-Anne could run an analysis on the logo and find out more.

He was well-positioned to make a shot with his Electro-pistol at the roaming guard, but his angle was poor to the roof door and the helicopter shielded the other guards. He'd have to move.

Turnkey started to put away the handheld device, but stopped when the roof door slammed open in front of the helicopter. Out of the door came Alabaster Dangermond, slumped over the shoulder of one of the huge men Turnkey had seen in the apartment before the blinds were drawn.

He stayed down and watched his handheld as another of the men came through with the thief slumped over his shoulder. Next came the well-dressed man and the third bodyguard. The man in the white suit shielded his face with his hand to his forehead as he looked down, blocking the sunrays from his eyes.

Turnkey watched as the newcomers boarded the helicopter. Once onboard, the two remaining guards entered the aircraft.

The only option left was to disable the helicopter. Adjusting the voltage on the gun for maximum power, he peeked over the wall and aimed it at the helicopter, unloading three shots. The projectiles hit something before reaching the target. An invisible force field around the helicopter absorbed the streaks of electricity, making a blueish bubble appear all around the aircraft for a split second. It was unlike anything Turnkey had seen before. The Electro-pistol didn't slow the copter at all. It started to lift off the pad.

Thinking quickly, he aimed his watch at the copter and pushed a button. A magnetic homing beacon shot out of the watch and flew toward the helicopter. The blades from the flying machine altered its course, but it passed through the force field and hit the outer hull, sticking to the exterior.

The pilot looked at Turnkey and rotated the machine toward the agent. He jumped on to the rappelling rope and started down. Ignoring him now, the helicopter rose into the air and turned in a southerly direction, rising higher and higher into the air as it flew away.

Turnkey finished the quick descent down the side of the building and mounted his motorcycle. He linked the watch interface with his helmet display to track the helicopter.

"Okay Bike, chart the fastest route to the homing beacon and call HQ." He took off on the motorcycle, following the fastest path.

The bike connected him with Chin Chin.

"Sensei Xu, Alabaster has been captured. He broke into the thief's apartment but a man showed up and captured him. I'm pursuing them right now and I've called for backup. I'm uploading all the video data I have."

The martial arts master came through on audio. "Yes, Agent Keystone, we are receiving your intel upload right now. Can we offer assistance? Where is the helicopter going?"

"I think it's headed to the International Airport. Can

you have it grounded? The registration number was not visible. Check the crescent moon insignia from the video."

"I will see what we can do. Keep us informed, Agent Keystone," said the Chinese man. "We will update your backup with the intel. Over and out."

Turnkey drove rapidly through the streets of Astana in the direction of the airport. He swerved in and out through the traffic, until he hit the highway. Then he crushed his throttle and hit speeds of 100 miles per hour on the straight road.

Hold on, Al. I'm coming for you.

The tracking device showed the helicopter had come to a stop at an outer hangar at the international airport.

Turnkey arrived in less than ten minutes. The outer hangar was unguarded and its main bay door was closed.

He parked near the side door and drew his Electro-pistol. The side door was unlocked and he quietly opened it and went inside. In front of him were crates of stacked aviation equipment blocking the view of the copter. He peeked around and saw the same helicopter he'd been tracking.

Some men were sitting at a table near the back wall of the hangar playing cards and talking in Russian. Their guns were lying next to them in a heap.

Turnkey came in unnoticed and snuck around to the closed hangar door. Using the craft as a shield, he moved closer and peered into the helicopter window. It was abandoned. Alabaster was gone. He thought for a moment, grabbed the small magnetic homing beacon, and then charged at the men playing cards at the table.

Pointing his gun at them he said, "Kuda oni delis?"

The guards froze and immediately raised their hands. He again repeated the phrase, this time in English, "*Where did they go?*"

One with a fat nose and stubble for a beard spoke up. "Zey tooks za plane, da," he said as he pointed out to the runway beyond the hangar bay.

It was Turnkey's worst nightmare. He had to find the plane.

Looking at the men he said, "Dos Vidaniya!" and rapidly shot each of them with his Electro-pistol, knocking all four men out cold, leaving them to sleep like little babies.

Turnkey rushed out the door of the hangar and looked at the planes taking off. He spun around trying to find it.

There.

A small jet with the same crescent moon logo as the helicopter was taxiing onto the main runway, readying for take-off. The plane came to a stop and sat on the landing strip.

He started running toward it at a full sprint but before he could get close, the jet launched forward for takeoff, rising up into the air.

Turnkey slowed down, his arms flailing. Defeated. He quickly made a call with his watch to contact HQ.

"Sensei Xu, can you see Al's VT? Is his tracker working?" he said, out of breath.

The Chinese man spoke loudly, "No. His VT turned off 40 minutes ago. What has happened, Agent Keystone?"

The agent explained what transpired just as the two

senior U.S.A. agents parked their car next to his motorcycle near the hangar. Then out of the hangar, the copter rose and flew away. All evidence of the abduction was gone. And with it, Alabaster Dangermond.

32

Darjeeling

Moonshae smiled as he ascended into the air on his private jet. His plan was coming together, and now he had Alabaster Dangermond. With the skills of Katya and Alabaster at his disposal, there was nothing to keep him from his treasure. All of the stones would soon be in his possession and his machine would be complete.

The jet moved at supersonic speed as it pierced the air just beyond Mach 3 toward Dr. Zerick Moonshae's villa situated on the secluded island. In only a few hours' time, they had arrived.

Flying into his private hidden landing strip built into the side of the island mountain, the jet came to a halt as the hangar bay door closed, concealing the large opening from the world. Lights illuminated the interior hangar bay that contained more than a few aircraft, all hidden away from any boats that might be near the island.

Moonshae treasured his privacy and this place had plenty of it. In the heart of the mountain was the landing strip and many hidden passages led up to the huge mansion built into the side of the mountaintop. As was custom, Willoughby stood at the bottom of the jet stairs with a silver platter and hot tea.

"Ah, Willoughby. Thank you. Thank you," Dr. Z. said to his butler as he sipped on the scalding Darjeeling tea that always greeted him when back from trips. He was particular about having Darjeeling upon returns.

The servant bowed to his master. "I trust your trip was a success, sir?"

The boss looked up at the plane. "Oh, yes, Willoughby, oh, yes." Two of the bodyguards emerged carrying Katya and Alabaster, who were both still knocked out by sleeping drugs, down the stairs of the jet.

The man sipped more of his hot tea. "Is the chamber ready?"

"Exactly to your specifications, sir."

"Good….good. Very good. Have these two moved to the chamber while I finish my tea. I want you to see personally to the map, Willoughby."

"Right away, sir."

~

Turnkey sat on the plane flying back to New York City.

"Well, have you figured out anything?" he asked.

He could see the team at HQ gathered in the Yellow Level Briefing Room from the secure video line on the company jet.

Mary-Anne answered first. "No. The insignia is a mystery. All searches failed. However, the registration numbers on the jet came up connected to a corporation in Zurich, Switzerland, called Moon International. But they don't use that crescent moon insignia."

The Chief looked around the room. "What do we know about Moon International?" Perkins brought the Chief some tea.

"Not much, Chief," said Sensei Xu. "Moon International provides relief aid to developing countries—they help the needy around the world. They also deal in a variety of investments. They like to own land, and records indicate they have land holdings in almost 170 countries."

Turnkey shook his head. "Whoa! That's almost all the countries in the world. What do they do with all that land, Sensei Xu?"

The Chinese sage stroked his white beard. "We do not know the answer to this puzzle. It will take a while for us to piece together that intel using satellite imagery. Initial views show a similar-looking communication structure on each of their properties, but we do not know its function or purpose. Once we identify the geographic locations of all their land, we can run an analysis of land use."

The Chief put down his teacup. "How long will that take?"

"Just a couple of days, Chief," said Mary-Anne.

The Chief turned to look at Turnkey on the video screen. "In the meantime, Agent Keystone, I am sending you to Switzerland to find out more about Moon International and why they might be holding one of my agents."

Turnkey nodded. "Okay, Chief. I'll alert the crew to the change in destination. Did the facial recognition from my video recording of the thief's apartment or the helipad come out?"

Mary-Anne stood up. "No, Turnkey. That well-dressed man knew what he was doing. He never once gave us a view of his face. He's a clever one." The girl sat back down and jotted a note to herself.

Turnkey looked off to the side at a computer. It showed the new details about the mission to Moon International in Zurich coming through from HQ. He looked back at the video screen. "Who's my contact in Switzerland?"

Sensei Xu spoke, "Look for a man dressed in all black with a red pen in his left pocket sitting at the Schwarzwald Café in downtown Zurich. Prompt him with the code words in the mission brief."

Turnkey let the pilots know they should change course and head to Zurich, Switzerland.

In the cargo bay of the aircraft sat the agents' motorcycles. Before the flight out of Astana, Turnkey had returned to Katya's building rooftop to recover Al's gear and he used the auto-pilot on the motorcycle to get it back to the plane. Now he wished he could recover his friend, too.

33

Manners

Alabaster Dangermond's eyes opened very slowly. He was groggy from the injection he had been given in the thief's apartment. Everything hurt—everything. He was sitting on a comfortable chair. The shapes in front of him were multiple shades of blue, brown, and tan, but he couldn't make them out in the dim light. Closing his eyes again, he wished for sleep. He had a feeling he was not alone, but he fell back asleep anyway.

"Mr. Dangermond? Mr. Dangermond? It is time for you to wake up."

Where have I heard that voice before?

Al opened his eyes. Near him was the well-dressed man from the thief's apartment sitting in a chair. Behind him were shelves of books, hundreds, maybe thousands, of them. Looking around he saw the girl, Katya, slumped over in a blue chair like his.

"Ah, good. You are awake!" Moonshae said. "I am so

sorry to have had to knock you out. But of course it was for your own good."

Al felt stuck to the chair. *Can I move? Is there anything wrong with me?* Twitching his arm and his leg, he was perfectly capable of moving, even though his body ached from all the tumbles and the shock it had received. Moonshae got a little closer.

"Tell me, Mr. Dangermond, what do you think of my little study, hmm?"

With everything his muscles could give, Alabaster exploded his body out of the chair to attack Moonshae! Rising up and diving toward the man he hit an invisible force field that reverberated blue when struck. It pushed him back down onto the ground with a thud.

Dr. Z laughed. "Oh, yes! You've found my protective shield! I'd recommend you hold yourself back or you might find it too painful to continue here in my study."

Al was exhausted. He moved from the floor and sat back down. Moonshae sat in the same kind of chair as Al and the thief. Next to Moonshae was a table with a large unrolled map resting on top, and next to it, the Serpent's Blade.

"Hmmm… Let's awaken dear Katya now. Oh, Katya! Dear Katya, it is time to wake up," the older man said. She awoke slowly and moved her hands up to her neck to rub the back of it.

"What's the deal, Moonshae?" Katya asked. She was clearly annoyed with her new surroundings.

Al saw the look of confusion and fierceness in her eyes

as she stared at Dr. Moonshae. He thought she might attack him too.

"Don't even try, sister. We're surrounded by force fields." Al stretched over the armrest and flicked the force field with his finger, revealing it to her.

Al looked back at the boss. "Why are we here, Moonshae?"

"You are here, Mr. Dangermond, because I have a job for you." Moonshae stood up and raised his arms. "You see, in all my years of research and study, I have discovered countless numbers of secrets. Secrets of the past, secrets of the future, and secrets of the here and now. The world is my playground, Mr. Dangermond, and you and Katya are my helpers."

This guy is insane.

Moonshae walked over to the map. "You see, I've discovered something extraordinary. It is so special that I hesitate to even let you in on this little secret of mine. But alas, I must! My map here is quite ancient and I can't dare tell you where it comes from. But what part of my secret I can say, is that it tells me where all my trinkets of curiosity are hidden throughout the world." Moonshae reached over and moved his fingers over to the flat part of the Serpent's Blade.

"I would like you to retrieve the Alexandrian Lamp from the famous Louvre art museum in Paris, France. And Katya, you will join him."

"Ha, ha. You must be joking! What a funny fellow you are, Dr. Zerick Moonshae!" Al began to mock him. "You are totally crazy."

"Do not call me crazy!" Moonshae yelled back as he spun around. Al had hit a soft spot. Moonshae paused and fixed his mussed hair. He took a deep breath. "My apologies. 'Manners maketh man.' Please excuse me for that tirade. I lost my temper and I failed to show you nice manners. I do detest yelling." He adjusted his tie and cleared his throat.

"Mr. Dangermond. You and Katya will retrieve the Alexandrian Lamp for me from Paris. I have arranged everything for you. I ask that you leave as soon as you've prepared." Moonshae sat down in his chair.

"Let me get this straight, boss. You hired her and she stole the blade for you. You snatched me and knocked me out. You brought us here and surrounded us with force fields and now you want us to go on our way to recover some artifact for you from Paris? Does that about sum it up?"

"Yes, Mr. Dangermond. That is it, precisely. I see you catch on quickly."

"Yeah, well…about that… How about…no."

Moonshae smiled at him. "I thought you might say that. Please reconsider."

"Why would I ever work for you? You murdered my parents, sent me a video of my parents' death, kidnapped me, and now you want me to work for you? Are you insane?"

"Well, Mr. Dangermond, it is actually quite simple. You will work for me because I've asked you to."

Al stood up and felt the pain in his legs. "I'll never work for you, Moonshae."

"Ah, never say never, Mr. Dangermond."

And with that Dr. Zerick Moonshae stood up and walked

over to a panel of books, pressed one of the spines, and opened the entire wall. He walked through the exit and the panel closed, leaving Alabaster and Katya alone with the map and the sword and shelves of books.

Al sighed. Then collapsed into his chair. After a while, he fell asleep again.

34

Zip Line

There.

Turnkey walked right up to the man in black sitting at the table. He had a red pen in his left pocket at the outdoor Schwarzwald Café in downtown Zurich.

"Pardon me, but what an unusual pen you have. Do you always go out with it?"

Turning the page of his newspaper, the man looked up at him. "Only when the weather is nice."

The two acknowledged each other with slight head nods.

Turnkey put his hand on the empty chair. "May I sit down?"

"Yes, please join me." The man continued to read his paper and Turnkey sat down.

Very quietly, the teen agent asked, "What do you have for me?"

The man folded up his newspaper. "Perhaps we should find a more secluded location to chat. Over your left shoulder, do you see the two men at the counter eating?"

Turnkey signaled for the waiter to come over as he looked at the two men sitting at the counter. They didn't look in his direction.

The waiter arrived and Turnkey asked him for a drink in a to-go cup. As the waiter walked away, he looked at the man with the red pen. "Who are they?"

The man leaned in. "I don't know, but they've been trailing me all around Zurich this morning and I haven't been able to shake them."

The waiter brought Turnkey a drink and the Zurich agent paid the bill. The two agents left the café. They walked down the street to a park filled with walking paths, benches, men playing chess on outdoor tables, and pigeons—standard European fare. They talked quietly as they strolled.

"The Moon International building in Zurich is that taller black one to your right, just beyond the park, Agent Keystone. I'm familiar with some of its structure, but I have never been inside." Pigeons moved out of their way as they walked along the path.

"Did you get me an appointment, so I can get inside?"

"No Agent Keystone. The soonest I could get an appointment anywhere near the communication center on the upper floors was four days from now."

Turnkey gave him a sharp look. "Four days? That won't

work. Can you get me close enough to hack into their computer network from another place?"

The man's face dropped. "I'm afraid not. Their building is built like an embassy—they're bullet, sound, and communication proofed. The only way to hack into their system is to be inside the building. Although the appointment is in four days, HQ has authorized me to get you in sooner."

"Okay, what's the op?"

~

Alabaster awoke after several hours and felt a lot better. Katya stared at him.

He wiped the drool from the corner of his mouth and then began his investigation. He started by systematically testing the force field to find a way out. The space inside the force field was large enough for him to move around the chair and not much more.

He flicked the containment field showing the blue edge. Then he looked over at Katya. "So you work for *this* guy?"

"Not by choice. You should be careful. I've seen him dispose of more enemies than I care to count." She adjusted her position in the chair. "He will do anything to get his way. If you don't do this work for him, he will make you pay."

"Well, there is no way I'm working for this slime ball. And if you're not working for him by choice, I suggest you tell me how I can escape this blue containment field."

Al tried to move the chair but it was secured to the wood floor. "And what's with my parents? Why did he fake their death in the car wreck after I turned seven and then kill them later? Was it about *their precious stone*?"

"Talk to *him*, Dangermond," was all Katya would say about it.

As Al tested the force field, Katya looked at him and smiled. "There is no escape from his will. I've tried every scenario in my mind and there simply is no escape. Whatever Zerick Moonshae wants, he gets."

Al was getting tired again. He sat back down in his chair and thought for a long while. They said nothing to each other and silence filled the chamber.

Al sat up and put his hands on the arms of the chair, ready to hoist himself up. "Moonshae doesn't win this time!"

The agent stood up and moved behind the chair. He punched a hole in the rear of the high-back chair and broke through the fabric. He broke off part of the wood frame and found flat metal pieces inside. Taking the metal, he began to pry up the wood slats of the floorboards.

"See, told you!" Al said with a fist pump. He broke a hole in the floorboards to the room below the library. Once the hole was big enough to fit through, he shimmied down it into the room below.

Before he dropped he smiled at her.

The girl rolled her eyes. "Show off!"

Al lowered into a standard storage room. Boxes and crates were everywhere. Some of the boxes contained weapons, according to the markings on the box. Six long crates were marked as having missiles. Off to the side was a set of double-doors. Al opened the door into a hallway that led to a large elevator at the end. There were a couple of doors off the hallway and the first one he came to had a small glass pane in the door so he could see in.

As he looked into the room from the door, he saw the glass prison where his parents had been murdered years ago. *Moonshae.* A flood of emotion hit Alabaster as the images of the video came back into his mind. Instead of sadness, his chest felt hot with anger.

Al tried the other doors but they were all locked, so he went to the elevator. The elevator doors opened with a push of a button and he went in. There were 12 floor buttons; Al pushed 'Floor 1 - House' and hoped for the best. It started up. Dr. Zerick Moonshae would never see him coming.

$\sim$

Turnkey looked across the expanse and pulled the trigger.

Out of his gun shot a black four-pronged grappling hook with an attached cable. It hit the roof of the Moon International building. Turnkey clipped the special gun back into the winch manifold and pushed the reverse button on the winch to which the cable was attached. The cable became taught as the grappling hook latched onto a concrete wall on the roof.

Turnkey turned to the agent with the red pen who helped him hook onto the cable. Looking at the man and smiling, he launched himself on the zip line under cover of night.

Landing on the opposite roof, he secured his harness

on the cable. Later, the winch would pull him back up the cable after he retrieved any data on Al.

Turnkey easily picked a roof door security lock. He examined the lock when the door was open and it was not electrified—no alarm system was connected to the door. He was in.

He carefully walked through the complex checking for cameras and laser beams, but he found only a few and they were easily avoided. Turnkey looked for the most likely computer candidate to try to hack. At the uppermost level of the building there were few offices but still enough computers. He decided to hack the Senior Branch manager's office, someone by the name of Mr. Gooks, who probably had high-level access to secure files with his login.

"Here's to you, Mr. Gooks," Turnkey said as he inserted his small digital drive into the slot on the keyboard to assist him breaking the man's password. Gooks only used a simple password 'skooG'—his name backwards. *Mary-Anne is a dream creating all this tech.*

As he searched the computer network, he quickly located top-secret Moon International files, but nothing stood out linked to the Serpent's Blade or Tokyo. What he did find were files on Thomas and Cynthia Dangermond. *Why does Moon International have files on Alabaster's parents?* At that moment, he felt something hot on his neck and then he fell out of the chair. The last thing Turnkey saw before he blacked out were two men in dark clothes looking down at him as he lay on the floor.

~

Al reached the top floor. Unlike the darkened elevator, the door opened to the magnificent rays of the sun. He stepped into a large atrium with glass windows everywhere and furniture of colorful design. To the left and the right, interconnected rooms seemed to go on forever. The view of the ocean surprised him and the spectacular scene made him pause. Al could feel the warm breeze and smell the sea salt from the water.

"Do you like it?" came the all-too-familiar voice from behind him.

"Do you like the view?" Moonshae asked again.

Al could see he was not armed. Now was his chance.

The villain raised his finger. "Mr. Dangermond, let me caution you in your next choice of action. You can either hear me out or I shall have to put you back in the study with Katya." Al wanted to apprehend this man but he also wanted to know why his parents had been killed. He decided to hear Zerick Moonshae out—for now.

The man gestured to the wicker chairs in the room. "Please have a seat."

"I'll stand, Moonshae." Al crossed his arms in front of his chest.

Zerick Moonshae moved over to a spot behind the wicker chairs and began to pace. "Very well. You've been knocked out for three days now since we departed Astana. And much has occurred. I've asked you to help me with a mission in Paris but you've said no. I was hoping you would just say yes, seeing how powerful I am. I saw through your little trick of invisibility, you know. But now you've broken out of my force field in my make-shift library—very impressive, Mr. Dangermond."

Al shifted his weight.

"Now, I must insist that you work for me." Moonshae used a remote and turned on the multiple large screen televisions mounted on the walls of the room.

Turnkey was on each monitor hanging upside down by his feet.

"Turnkey! Why you—"

He dove toward Moonshae, and then froze in mid-air.

"Ah, Ah! Do you think I am stupid, Mr. Dangermond?" Moonshae shook his finger at him and pointed to a small remote device in his other hand.

Al floated three feet off the ground, stretched out and motionless. He could think, he could breathe, he even could move his eyes, but he could not move his body. It was an odd sensation, like being up against a wall, but nothing was there.

"Say hello to my nanotech," said Moonshae. "My little nanites can do wonders. They can blot out the Astana sunlight, they can create force fields, and most certainly they can kill you, Agent Dangermond, if it is my will."

Moonshae's tone turned from playful to serious. "Now, Mr. Dangermond. Please observe. If you choose not to work for me, well, I am afraid it is the end for your friend." The television zoomed out and Al could see his partner dangling over a tank of bubbling chemicals.

"One push of the button and your friend will take a dunk," Moonshae said. "Now that I have your undivided attention again, Mr. Dangermond, will you complete my mission to Paris?"

Al had taken hostage training at the Agency, but nothing prepared him for this. The closest training to this scenario told him that he could sacrifice himself to save the life of a fellow agent. If he went with Moonshae, he would be sacrificing his character and what he stood for.

As Al floated motionless in the air from the nanotech support, he could feel the rage welling up inside of him. The man before him was the murderer of his parents. A criminal who deserved justice. And if Al didn't act, murderer of his best friend.

"I despise you, Moonshae. You're going to lose," Al said. Then he sighed. "I'll do what you want in Paris on two conditions—tell me what you want the Serpent's Blade for, and tell me what my parents have to do with this. Why did you murder them?"

"Ah, the negotiator! Good, very good, Mr. Dangermond. Now that's the spirit! Agreed. I will let you know these few little secrets, but only if you agree to do everything I ask of you. After all, Paris is just the beginning."

35

Vikings

Ding. The elevator doors opened to the first floor and out stepped a butler, two guards, and the girl with the sword.

"Katya! Yes, please, over here." Moonshae ushered her to take a seat near Alabaster as he took the sword from her and the map from Willoughby. When she sat down, her auburn hair blew over and clipped Al on the shoulder. He willingly sat in his chair, no longer under the influence of the nanotech.

Moonshae cleared his throat. "You, my friends, are on a fantastic journey with me. Scattered throughout the world are my precious treasures. You are tasked to bring them back to me. I will, of course, pay you well. For you, Katya, your standard rate, and for you, Mr. Dangermond—well, I will pay you handsomely, as well."

Disgusted by Moonshae, Al determined to find out everything he could. Every detail was important and might give him an advantage to save Turnkey. "What do you want with the treasures, Moonshae? Why are they important?"

"Perceptive question! You see, my young man, once there was a man just like you and me, well…more like me. He was a king. And he ruled the Vikings—"

"King Olaf," Al said. "The Viking King."

Moonshae smiled. "Indeed! But just before he became king, he visited a mysterious man called The Seer, on the Scilly Isles, southwest of England in the sea. The Seer was reported to know all things and predicted something of Olaf's future. You see, he told him that his men would mutiny against him and how it would happen. And afterwards, Olaf would convert to Christianity. After leaving The Seer, that is exactly what happened."

Moonshae's eyes widened. "He sailed away and became a glorious Viking king for many years, defending his Norwegian homeland from invaders until the battle of battles."

Katya yawned.

Moonshae continued his enthusiastic lecture. "In the year 1000, King Olaf's enemies sailed to intercept him and his ships in the Baltic Sea. Surprising them with a fleet of seventy ships, they came upon Olaf's eleven ships. Although overwhelmed by the odds, it was a fierce battle and the seventy took heavy casualties. But, one by one, Olaf's ships fell to his enemies. The royal ship, the Long Serpent, was the greatest Viking ship ever built. It had 34 rooms and was the most powerful ship in the sea. After a long-fought battle, the King recognized defeat and jumped from the bow of the ship into the cold Baltic waters. His heavy royal armor made him sink deeper and deeper, but according to my source, he held his breath and threw off his body gear. His death was pronounced and he was never seen again."

Moonshae drank from his cup of water and turned his back on the two onlookers. He lowered his voice, "Even though he was pronounced dead, he lived on in seclusion and secrecy. Secret gifts were sent to the ruler of the lands of England, Ethelred the Unready, and to King Olaf's sister, Astrid, in Norway, and many pondered if he was still alive. Reports heralded Olaf sightings throughout the known world, but I alone know where he was and what he was doing. Through my detailed research and careful study, I have discovered his handwritten journals…and…they reveal all."

Moonshae gazed off into the distance. "Olaf returned to The Seer and had but one passion until his death, to know how The Seer knew the future. And Olaf discovered The Seer's secret, but wrote in a journal that the secret was too terrible to put to pen, for fear that others might discover it later. He wrote that if one were to solve the mystery, he would be worthy to wield the secret of The Seer."

Moonshae pointed to the table. "He left us—well, me—a puzzle, a map. My map. Now, you see, Mr. Dangermond and Ms. Volkoff."

Al looked a Katya.

Moonshae raised his eyebrows. "Yes, Katya *Volkoff*…"

The man cleared his throat. "Now, as I was saying, Olaf

left me this map. It has taken me years of study to under-stand its cryptic nature. The man took treasures to remote places on Earth and used this map to describe what was sent and where it was left."

"The Serpent's Blade," Al said aloud.

"Precisely." Moonshae held up the blade of Olaf Tryg-gvason into the air.

"Fine, Moonshae. You want us to get you Olaf's things. But why?"

Moonshae laughed at him. "Well…to put together the secrets of The Seer."

Al stood up. "Let me get this straight. You want me and Katya to go to Paris to get this lamp and bring it back to you, or else you'll do away with my friend—because it's connected to some thousand-year-old dead dude?"

"And my sisters," Katya added, as she looked away from Dr. Moonshae.

Al looked toward Katya as he sat back down. *So that's why she works for him. He has her sisters.*

Moonshae pushed his fingers together in a sort of trian-gle shape in front of him. "Yes, I am afraid so. I do detest violence, but nevertheless, when one is discovering the important secrets of the world…" He moved toward the map and looked over it.

"You see, Mr. Dangermond, I am not your enemy. On the contrary, I am the true steward of human knowledge. Knowledge is a commodity and I have vault-loads of it. Lack of knowledge is your only enemy."

Moonshae's self-importance disgusted Al, but he was

stuck. If he tried to stop Dr. Z., it meant the end of his friend. If he helped Moonshae, he would be breaking every law and oath he had sworn to uphold for the sake of justice. He would be helping the murderer who had caused him so much pain.

"What of my parents? How are they involved in this? Why did you kill them?"

"Well, Mr. Dangermond, your parents had one of Olaf's treasures. Didn't you know that? They had a special stone, which surely you now possess and which we will soon retrieve, also."

How could they have a treasure from a dead Viking king?

Al stood up and clenched his fists. "So that's why you killed them? Why you sent me the video? So I would go looking for it?"

"They wouldn't give it to me, so I moved on to their only son. I've been waiting to find you, so you could find it for me, since they proved to be so unhelpful."

Al gave him a sharp look and gritted his teeth. "You're sick, Moonshae. You've ruined my life. And now you're trying to ruin it more. I'll keep my word, but I'm going to stop you."

Dr. Z. looked at Al and grinned. "We will see, Mr. Dangermond. Do I need to resort to this despicable violence with your partner? Are you lying, or will you really keep your word?"

"Yes, I've given you my word, but you still disgust me."

Moonshae smiled at Al. "So, first we will go to Paris. And after, we will explore your family possessions." Then the man walked over to the window and breathed the sea air deeply into his lungs.

Al sat in his seat and looked at Turnkey dangling for his life. He *had* to save him.

"Alabaster," Zerick said. Al turned to look at him. "If you reveal to your U.S.A. friends what you are doing, or if you have any contact whatsoever with your colleagues, your friend gets the plunge. Do I make myself clear?"

Al glared at him. "Yes. But you're still going to lose." Al saw Katya staring at him, and then she looked away.

Moonshae waved a hand of dismissal toward Al. "Once my precious treasures are recovered—*all* my precious treasures—you may have your friend back…and your sisters." He turned toward Katya. "Please follow me."

36

Parisian Date

Amsterdam, Netherlands
52.307653 N, 4.982769 E

"Agent Martinez, I think I've found him," said the youth, not more than twelve years old. He was looking across the room at Mary-Anne on Orange level.

She walked over and looked at the analysis and map on the screen. The Trainee had put together some nice work. His analysis extrapolated where Agent Turnkey Keystone might be.

"How did you determine this place, Xander?"

The boy looked back at his computer screen. "Well, we knew that Agent Keystone was taken here to Amsterdam based on his VT transmitter." He pointed on the map near the waterfront. "They took the light rail line 54 and we lost him here." The young agent pointed to the southern part of the city.

"If we extrapolate from the end of the 54 line to the last location we tracked, here, and apply some map math, Agent Keystone should be somewhere in this area." The Trainee pointed to a specific location in southern Amsterdam.

Mary-Anne looked at him. "Why that area?"

"That area is Gaasperpark. I cross-referenced the Moon International land holdings in Amsterdam near Agent Keystone's last know location. This structure, here, is owned by Moon International." The youth zoomed into the buildings just northwest of the park on his computer.

A smile came across her lips. "Brilliant work."

~

PARIS, FRANCE
49.012150 N, 2.499863 E

Al opened his eyes.

A man in a white coat pulled back the needle and syringe. "Give it a few minutes before za medicine vers off. Soon you will feel vell." He had been knocked out again by Moonshae as a precaution at the secret island base. Dr. Z. obviously didn't want him to know where it was located.

Al felt the jolt as the jet touched down on the runway. "Paris. It's 7 PM." The short statement came over the speaker in the jet.

The plane came to a stop. From behind, Al heard a familiar voice. "Let's go, Dangermond," Katya said, as she walked past him and down the exit stairs. Al got up and followed her into a large hangar. Supposedly this was Paris, France, but no one greeted them. Apparently, they were able to bypass immigration and customs—no doubt due to Moonshae's illegal abilities. Al felt groggy from the knockout injection.

Katya walked briskly over to a black van with dark tinted windows and looked it over. She pointed to the back of the van and turned to Al. "Check the gear."

Al shrugged his shoulders and jumped into the back and started the inventory check. Katya hopped into the driver's seat and started the vehicle.

"Be thorough, Dangermond. If we're missing anything, we can get it at one of Moonshae's safe houses, downtown." Adjusting the rearview mirror, she drove off toward the Louvre in downtown Paris. Satisfied they had the gear they needed, Al moved to the front of the van and sat in the passenger seat.

It was dusk as they drove from the southern outskirts, northward from the airport into the city streets of Paris. Coming from the south, they took the larger boulevards toward the giant Eiffel Tower inside the heart of downtown.

Crossing the famous River Seine at the Pont Royal Bridge, Katya drove past the Tuileries Gardens and then west past the largest Ferris wheel in France. Alabaster had read about it and hoped one day he could ride the 200-foot tall wheel. The sight of something familiar made him feel better. He wondered how Turnkey was doing.

Coming to the large intersection at the Place de la

Concorde, which connected at the other end to Napoleon's monumental Arc de Triumph via the wide avenue of the Champs-Élysées, Katya parked the van just off to the side and the newly minted partners began their wait until after midnight—the time they would jump into action. Although the van sat out in the open pointed toward their target past the gardens, the busy intersection concealed their stakeout.

Al thought Katya seemed in a bad mood, between the silence and short commands she barked, so he sat there studying the Louvre on a tablet. After a while he needed a break and hoped she was feeling more sociable, so he put down the tablet and looked at her. "So Moonshae has your sisters, like he has Turnkey?"

"Why do you care?"

"Well, just making small talk, I guess."

Katya stared out of the van and said nothing.

Al looked out at the people riding the Ferris wheel. The lights made it sparkle in the dark. Again, he turned to Katya. "I guess I thought maybe we had that in common—anyway, we have a while to wait so I thought we'd talk about *something*."

"Look, Dangermond, I'm not your friend, and yes, Moonshae has my sisters. He's in charge for now. Okay? Is that enough for you?"

"Whoa. Hey, I'm just trying to pass the time. If you don't want to talk about it, that's fine with me."

"No. I don't want to talk about it. Just concentrate on the mission, Dangermond."

That was the end of the conversation.

Al picked the tablet back up and studied the schematics of the Louvre floor plans. From the intel provided by Moonshae, the lamp was cataloged and displayed in the Egyptian section.

After about an hour, Katya turned and looked at Al. "Okay, Dangermond, I'm sorry. Look, we're probably going to zip around the world for Moonshae, so we might as well be on the same page. He's the only person to catch me stealing. He imprisoned me and then forced me to steal for him while he holds my sisters hostage. I don't want to talk about my sisters, so don't bring them up again. Let's just stick to our plans and get this lamp and the other stuff for him so we can move on."

Al nodded. "Okay, agreed."

He knew there was more to this girl than she would have him believe. In the dungeon interrogation room of the Dragon's Lair in Tokyo, he had recognized her pain. And now he knew Moonshae held her sisters ransom, forcing Katya to do his dirty work of thievery around the world. Al couldn't help but think of the motto of the U.S.A.—to silently save the world, one person at a time. Maybe he could help Katya save them, too, after saving Turnkey.

People began filling the streets now that it was dark. Musicians, dancers, and a whole assortment of people milling about on the Champs-Élysées. The large Ferris wheel lights were mesmerizing as they spun around and around for its riders. Lights filled the Place de la Concorde and illuminated the Egyptian obelisk from Luxor, given to the city over a century ago.

As he sat there, watching people and cars pass by around and around the Place de la Concorde, Al thought about his interactions with Katya. *There is good in her, I know it. Maybe she might join me against Moonshae…*

Al felt a hard nudge from Katya's elbow. "Wake up, Dangermond, it's time. What's the best approach to the roof?"

37

Art of the Steal

In the dark, Al led Katya on foot through the gardens to the Louvre Museum's eastern building. The museum complex had many buildings and wings, and each building had multiple levels filled with the world's greatest art and treasure. The Louvre was one of the most important museums in the world.

Concealed by the darkness, they scaled the building, with all kinds of black straps wrapped around their bodies. Katya had taught Al how to use the straps with suction cups before they left Moonshae's hideout. She made it to the top much faster than Al.

On top of the roof, Katya used her flashlight with two quick bursts of light toward the street. "Okay, Moonshae's goons have been alerted. They'll be ready to get us out of here once we get the lamp."

The pair made their way over to the spectacular glass ceiling. Using a combination of a suction cup and a diamond blade slicer, Katya created a hole near the metal supports that would allow her and Alabaster to descend into the building.

A similar laser protection grid like the one protecting the Shinjuku Tower windows in Tokyo also protected the Louvre, according to Moonshae's schematics. Katya pulled off her black belt and her backpack. Inside the pack were two unique crank devices. She mounted them on the outer glass on either side and they reached slightly over the edge of the cut hole. Taking the belt, she separated it into two strips, which became taut, and attached them with a small pole for each crank. It seemed to Al that Katya must have done this hundreds of times because she was fast and efficient.

Al whispered, "So, is this how you got into the Tokyo tower?" The thief nodded.

Katya misted some dust into the opening revealing the laser beams just below. "When I push this button, the cranks lower the belts right into the beams at the same time." She pushed the button and the belts lowered, cutting off the beam from both directions, leaving a hole for the thieves to drop into.

"Moonshae made these delicate, but flexible, black mirrors on the belt strips that absorb the laser beams. In about a minute, the beams will heat up the mirrors and send a feed-back loop right into the heart of the laser emitter. That usually shuts down the beams connected to those emitters. Once shut down, it's standard for the reboot cycle on these lasers to take about ten minutes before they come back on. The reboot is normal and doesn't report as a system malfunction." Katya pointed toward the sides of the wall where the emitters were located.

Katya moved a little closer to Al. "It always works for me, except when I do stupid things like in Tokyo. After I scaled the building outside and cut into the glass, I used these to stop the window sensors. But when I was in the ceiling, I accidentally crushed a couple of the black mirrors when I set my belt down while trying to lower the Serpent's Blade from its case. Since I couldn't escape back out the window without triggering the alarm, I had to wait for you to turn off the laser security net." Katya peered back down to see the action on the laser beams below and misted some more dust. After a moment, the beams disappeared. It had worked.

With the hole beam-free, Katya quickly dismantled the cranks and belts and put them back in her backpack and around her waist, respectively.

"Easy as that, Dangermond." The smirk was unmistakable, even in the dark.

On the edge of the cut glass, she put some sort of hard plastic edging all the way around on the inner side. Katya reached into the hole and mounted four suction cup carabineer hooks on the inner glass and slipped her straps into the hooks. With a little dive into the hole, she swung onto the ceiling, suspended by two of the hooks. Al followed.

Both of the thieves hung dangling from the hooks inside the Louvre's 30-foot ceiling.

Reaching back out of the hole, she carefully pulled the cut glass plate back into the hole from whence it came. The glass was supported by the hard plastic edging. Once in place, Katya checked the fit and pressed hard on one part of the plastic. It released a bluish tinted substance all the way around. Al thought it looked like a chemical released inside the plastic.

The plastic edging began to almost magically melt the glass back into form, concealing most of the original cut lines and leaving only a little white powder that was barely noticeable in the dim light from inside the museum.

"How did you do that?" Al whispered, now wondering what other kinds of little gadgets Katya had on her person.

She put a finger to her mouth. "Moonshae has some guy named Cy who makes this stuff… Now shut up or we are going to get caught."

The two intruders lowered themselves down to the Louvre floor. Al saw Katya press a button on her watch and the four hooks on the inner glass detached from the ceiling and floated down right into their hands. They refitted their straps and began the hunt for the lamp.

~

In the dark of night, six men emerged from the foliage of Gaasperpark. They cut through the metal fence and penetrated the grounds.

"Are you set?" Chin Chin Xu asked.

The commander looked at the Chinese man through his watch display and nodded. "Yes, sir, all rescue personnel accounted for. There is only one building with two guards outside. I see two mounted cameras over the door and they should be easy to destroy. What are your orders sir?"

"You are green-light-go, commander. Bring our man home!"

And with that, the U.S.A. commander and his five agents assaulted the Amsterdam Moonshae International complex with their heavy duty Electro-pistols to rescue Turnkey from Dr. Z's clutches.

38

Break

Egyptian caskets with mummies, carved stone tablets full of hieroglyphs, and massive numbers of gold and silver items lined the Louvre display cases.

Al looked at his watch. "We only have about four minutes until the camera system snapshots this room."

He had memorized the schedule of the security camera rotation that Moonshae had provided him. Every 15 minutes, two security cameras in each room snapped a picture for analysis. Supposedly, a computer algorithm compared the snapshots from all the Louvre rooms as it rotated through the different cameras in the museum. If the computer found an anomaly from the previous snapshot of the room, a guard would be alerted for further investigation before an alarm sounded.

Katya looked around. "Where is it?"

Al pointed to a series of four pedestals on one side of the room. On one of the four stands sat the Alexandrian Lamp under a thick glass case.

Al motioned toward her. "We don't have enough time before the camera captures us. Follow me."

Each of the cameras in the room had a limited field of view. The museum eliminated as many of the blind spots as possible, but a few remained. With the intel Moonshae provided, Al was able to identify the blind spots in this section. He told himself he would let the security museum staff know about the camera limitations once this was all over.

Katya followed Al to the corner of the room. He looked in the direction of the camera and moved her into place. She willingly obliged. They stood in the open, not covered by any obstruction.

Katya looked around the room. "Are you sure this is the spot, Dangermond?"

"Yes. The two cameras in this room don't cover this spot. But I'm going to have to hold onto you."

"Like…hug me?"

"Yeah."

"Fine, Dangermond."

Al adjusted her position slightly and then stood next to her. He wrapped his arms around her tightly. Her hair smelled like strawberries. They stood attached for about a minute in silence.

He let go of her. "Okay. The cameras have taken their shots."

Katya looked annoyed. "Let's get this thing and go, Dangermond."

They had 15 minutes to steal the lamp.

~

The commander burst into the detention room!

"Yo, I knew it." Turnkey got off the bed in the room. "I knew those were U.S.A. standard Electro-pistols. I could hear you using them from inside this cell!"

The commander surveyed the room and then turned to Turnkey. "Are you all right, sir? Are you fit to escape or do you need assistance?"

"I'm good, commander. Lead the way out." Turnkey gave one last look at the white room and then followed. The commander moved them rapidly down a hall, past guards knocked out on the ground, and out of the building. Turnkey breathed the free air deeply after his long days of incarceration.

~

Alabaster moved over to the pedestal that held the treasure. His research on the Alexandrian Lamp was extensive, given the short time he had. It was made of gold with a thick layer of lead inside the lamp. Its name came from its use at the Pharos Lighthouse in Alexandria, Egypt—one of the seven wonders of the ancient world. The lighthouse had stood for many centuries as the tallest structure on earth, and this lamp was used as part of the daily ritual. A caretaker would take the flame in the lamp from the bottom all the way up to the top, using it to ignite the fire of the famous lighthouse every night. After the destruction of the lighthouse, with all the warring in Europe through history, the lamp made its way northward to Viking territory, probably because of its utility—but maybe because of the superstitions surrounding it. Either way, it ended up a Viking possession. It looked smaller than what Al's research documents had shown.

He pointed to the bottom of the glass. "Look, here at the base. That's an alarm sensor. The glass is easy enough to lift off, but once we do, it will set off the alarm because of the pressure sensor on the pedestal."

Al adjusted his watch and used his laser to fry the small computer chip pressure sensor. Moonshae had given Al back his watch for the missions but told him to refuse contact from his superiors, or Turnkey would suffer the consequences. Dr. Z's engineers had disabled the communication protocol on the watch, just as a precaution. Al guessed they probably ripped off the design to reengineer their own version of the watch.

Satisfied the chip was destroyed, Al and Katya put on gloves and carefully lifted up the glass from the pedestal and set it on the ground. Alabaster took his small flashlight and inspected the lamp on the stand but did not see any additional security measures.

Reaching into his backpack, he pulled out something that looked like a spray paint canister. Popping off the top, he started to spray the lamp with a foaming substance. The foam began to quickly expand and harden.

"This stuff better protect the lamp like Moonshae said it would."

Katya opened Al's empty backpack. "It will. It creates a nice bouncy sponge inside the hard outer shell. I've used it before. On a job for Moonshae, an item slipped out of my hands and fell over a hundred feet without any damage at all."

Al carefully lifted the foam-sealed lamp from the stand, sprayed the bottom to finish the job, and put it in his backpack as Katya kept the bag open. They put the glass back on the pedestal, put away their gloves, and the two thieves made their way through the exhibit exit toward their escape point out of the museum. Al looked at his watch. They had eight minutes before the next photo of the room occurred.

They moved through the rest of the Egyptian and Greek rooms full of treasures and made their way down a set of stairs to the first floor. With all the Louvre history around him, he thought about the treasured stone that his parents supposedly had that Moonshae wanted.

Before they exited the stairwell onto the first floor, Al stopped.

"Katya, what if we joined forces against Moonshae? If you help me rescue my friend, I will help you. We can stop his toying with our lives."

She shook her head. "Shut up, Dangermond. Let's get going."

Al stayed put. "Come on, I'm serious. You're strong. We can beat him."

"Look, Dangermond. I told you he always gets his way. He messes with you because he can. You can't beat him. You don't get it. Now, let's go."

Al didn't move. "No. We can help each other. We can beat him at his own game."

Katya scrunched her nose. "Hey, we've all had loss in our lives. You think my parents hung around and helped me and my sisters out? Get over it. I mean, at least you've got a chance to see your parents again. I don't even know if my sisters are alive."

"What do you mean, *I have a chance to see my parents again*?"

Katya sighed. "Come on, Dangermond. Are you so dense? Moonshae is always talking in riddles. The guy is crazy from all the hours in his books."

Al stood waiting. He thought Katya might punch him.

She crossed her arms. "You're really thick. Fine. Moonshae put your parents in cryo-freeze. He showed me on a screen in his library when I brought the sword to him. They're still alive. Duh?"

"What?!" Al shouted.

At that moment, the entire museum exploded with blaring alarms.

39

Skunky

Al darted after Katya, who was already through the next exhibit doorway heading to their exit point. Flashing lights whirled around and around inside the museum. Al heard guards shouting; they were getting closer to him. He felt like panicking. If he was caught, Turnkey was dead.

He came to the stairs that led down to the basement cafeteria area and descended the steps. Halfway down the steps on a flat landing, he found Katya picking a lock to a wooden door.

She made quick work of it and the two went through the door and shut and locked it. They stood on a spiral staircase made of black metal that wound its way down. Katya led the way down and before they reached the bottom, she shot her weapon, destroying the security camera before they could be seen. In front of them was a door.

"Alabaster, get that door open!"

Above, he heard shouts and commotion from the army of security and police running around the museum.

Al broke the electronic cover plate off the wall to expose the electric panel and wires on the security lock. He was back at the Agent Trials. He jimmied the wires and started connecting them.

Katya stood at the base of the spiral staircase looking up with her non-lethal pistol, ready if the police came through. She had argued for a real gun, but Moonshae made her conform to Al's insistence on protecting civilians and security with a gun that deterred, not killed.

The projectiles for the gun were plastic bullets designed to flatten when they hit a person or objects—the plastic casing could be filled with anything.

"I'm putting in skunk bullets," Katya said.

Al knew she had a couple of different casings and now she chose a concentrated liquid skunk-spray extract. The bullets wouldn't kill anyone, but they would hurt and smell really bad, making the eyes swell up from the disgusting odor. Maybe the guards might even run away from the intense stench.

Still hidden in the stairwell, Al disconnected a couple of wires to splice them together. Connecting the blue and green wires set off a very loud alarm blaring in the room. Al wished Turnkey was here—he was so much better with electronics. The alarm was deafening, echoing off the walls. It was impossible to concentrate.

Covering his ears at the horrid sound, Al paused. Opening his eyes and uncovering his ears, he separated the wires and tried the blue with the ground. It did nothing. The police burst through the wooden door at the top of the spiral staircase. Katya started shooting and the police backed away from the open door as the entire stairwell began filling with skunk smell.

"Get that door open or we're both done! If you have any hope of seeing your friend—or your parents again—get us out of here, now!"

Al growled. "I'm doing the best I can!" The police dropped a canister down the staircase and it began to spew out gas.

Katya shot a few more blasts from her gun. "Knock out gas! Come on, get that door open!"

With tears in his eyes from the smell, Al focused amidst the loudness of the unbearable alarms. Katya started to cough from the gas. Al connected the white wire with the blue wire. The green light to the door came on and the heavy door opened.

Katya and Al ran through the heavy door into a docking area for boats to unload cargo from the river. A service boat was sitting next to the dock. The clean air began to flood Al's lungs and it felt reviving, but everything still smelled like skunk.

The plan was to get away by boat on the River Seine. Ahead of Al, at the end of the dock past the sliced metal fence, was the ride. Two of Moonshae's goons from the plane sat waiting on the boat. Katya dove through the small opening in the metal fence first and then Al followed.

Bullets from the police in the stairwell came whizzing by as the four criminals zoomed away in the boat. Al moved to the rear of the boat while the goons and Katya remained mid-ship, driving the speeding boat down the river. Al held on tight as he thought about his parents. He was going to find them and make Moonshae pay for what he had done.

French police cars could be seen and heard up on the bridges above them as the boat sped below on the river. It would only be a short time before the police helicopters would be scanning the river for them.

Al saw something flash from under his sleeve. It had to be from his watch. Pushing up his sleeve, he could see an incoming message. Moonshae's tech people were smart enough to shut off all communication features on his watch to prevent Alabaster from speaking or writing any details to the U.S.A., but somehow Mary-Anne had figured out how to send a message.

In the air above the boat, two helicopters emerged and began pursuing them on the river with high beam spotlights. Hearing the French police yelling for them to stop, the boat carried on, heading to one of Moonshae's safe houses along the river. Al saw Katya make a quick phone call.

While she was distracted, he looked down to read the individual, pixelated letters one at a time on his watch:

s.c.u.e.d.-.r.e.p.e.a.t.-.a.g.e.n.t.k.e.y.s.t.o.n.e.-.h.a.s.-.b.e.e.n.-.r.e.s.c.u.e.d.-.r.e.p.e.a.t…

40

Drips

Al turned off his watch display, breathing deeply as adrenaline rushed through his body. Turnkey was rescued.

Alabaster Dangermond sat on the back of the boat contemplating his decision. He could make the escape with the lamp, now that his friend was free. But his parents; he had to stay the course to rescue his parents.

What would they do?

They'd do their job. They'd risk everything to stop this maniac. They already had—they refused to give him the stone and they paid the price.

Looking around as the helicopters flew overhead, shining down their spotlights and shouting French commands over loudspeakers, Al saw the bend up ahead. It would be his best chance.

The motorboat banked to the left. Alabaster Danger-mond lifted himself up onto the edge of the craft. As the boat went under a bridge, he fell backwards overboard, splashing into the water.

"There! Dangermond just went overboard!" Katya yelled at the driver of the boat, pointing in his direction. The heli-copters continued with their spotlights on the boat—they missed his leap altogether because he had used the bridge to shield his escape.

Katya pushed into the driver and tried to take the wheel. She slowed the boat as Al made his way to the edge of the river under the bridge, still carrying the Alexandrian Lamp in his backpack.

The girl thief slowly turned the boat in the water, but one of the police helicopters flew right on top of them and shouted in French for them to give up. Al could see the angry grimace on her face as she slammed down the throttle and shot away from him with all the horsepower the twin engine motorboat could give. The other two men onboard fell backwards at the sudden acceleration. Alabas-ter Dangermond watched Katya and the goons disappear around the bend with the helicopters in hot pursuit—all hope to rescue his parents gone with them.

Hopping up onto the small walkway adjacent to the river edge, Alabaster walked from the river into the urban area of Paris. He felt tired and cold as he dripped the River Seine all over the sidewalks. He made his way to the CIA safe house in the city. All Junior Agents were required to memorize the location of various safe houses, which were located in major cities around the world.

Located down a poorly-lit alley in the arts district of the city, the secret agent walked up to the door on the side of the building. He pressed the call button next to the door.

"Identification?" the speaker said.

"Agent 18151721—Alabaster Dangermond requesting access."

...

...

"Access granted." Al heard a soft buzzing sound and the click of the door. He opened it and went into the safe house. He had made it.

~

Mary-Anne was the first at HQ to answer the call on the flat-panel screen. "Al! Are you all right?" Behind her on the vid, Al could see Sensei Xu, and it looked like the Chief had come down from his haunts to hear the news.

"Yeah, I'm okay and I've got the intel we need. But first, how is Turnkey? How did you find him?" Mary-Anne told him the details of the rescue and how they had tracked him using the VT to Amsterdam and saved him.

Alabaster ran his hand through his hair. "Hmm...I guess Moonshae doesn't know about the VT or he would have disabled it on Turnkey."

Sensei Xu popped his head into view. "Who is Moonshae,

Agent Dangermond? The man who kidnapped you in Astana?"

Alabaster filled him in on the details of what had happened in the Astana apartment with Dr. Zerick Moonshae and at the island mansion hideout. He described how Turnkey was used as leverage to get him to steal the Alexandrian Lamp and that Katya Volkoff was the name of the thief. He also told them about the Louvre, the escape, and that Katya said his parents were still alive.

Sensei Xu stroked his white beard. "And what of the Serpent's Blade?"

"I guess it's still with Moonshae in his mansion."

The Chief said something off-camera to Sensei Xu and then appeared on the screen. "What does he want with all of these treasures?"

Alabaster explained what Moonshae said about the stones and how they were connected to King Olaf. "United, they reveal a secret that Olaf was too afraid of, so he scattered them around the world, hidden in different treasures. Moonshae wouldn't tell me the secret, but he seems to know what it is."

The large man signaled Perkins to get him some tea. "And you say the stone your parents have is one of these Olaf treasures?"

"Yes, Chief. That's what Moonshae said."

Perkins was already there with tea for the man and he took a sip. "And Katya Volkoff confirmed they are alive, and you believe her?"

"Yes, sir. I don't know what would motivate her to lie about that."

The Chief looked around the room and then back at Al on the video screen. "Agent Dangermond. We have arranged for your flight out. Come back to HQ immediately and we can begin the analysis on the lamp. I will smooth things over with the French police authorities and the museum staff to borrow the lamp a little longer before we return it. I will also arrange to pay for all the damages to the museum. We will hunt down Dr. Moonshae and find out about your parents."

"Oh, Chief. Let the museum staff know we can give some pointers to upgrade their security measures." Al thought that little peace offering might go a long way for the Chief, who had to clean up this delicate bit of illegal activity.

As instructed, Al was taken by a local agent to the airport and boarded the plane in Paris. He flew back to New York City Headquarters. Exhausted, he slept the whole way back.

~

Al felt the aircraft touch down onto the runway. The sun shone into his window as it approached the U.S.A. hangar at J.F.K. International Airport. When the plane came to a stop inside the hangar, Turnkey was there waving at Al.

Turnkey jumped up and down when the aircraft door opened. "Al!"

"TK!" Al ran down the stairs from the plane and the

two clasped their right hands and gave a one-arm hug with their left arms.

"Yo! You all right, homie?"

Al nodded. "I'm good, bro, but that was crazy. How about you—are you all right? Moonshae is a scum for doing that to you."

Turnkey told Al about the incarceration and then Al told him about the nanotech.

"Oh, man, Al. That's advanced stuff. Mary-Anne doesn't even have that."

Al opened his backpack and showed Turnkey the encased treasure.

Turnkey scratched his head. "Yo, it doesn't look like much."

As they talked, Al saw Perkins walk into the hangar.

The skinny man stopped in front of them. "Agents! The Chief wants you on the chopper immediately." Perkins pointed out of the hangar and then looked down at his clipboard. "Well, what are you standing around for? Get a move on!"

The agents headed out of the hangar to the tarmac and got into the U.S.A. helicopter. Perkins arrived just a couple of minutes later and they departed. As they rose from the JFK airport, Al could see the dense traffic congestion of New York City below. He looked up and saw the downtown Manhattan skyline coming closer.

"I love this view," Al said. He pressed his nose to the glass. It was a clear sunny day in the city.

The helicopter flew over the East River just south of the

United Nations Building before landing next to the river on a helipad. The U.S.A. operated multiple helicopters and since the terrorist attacks of 2001, helicopters were not allowed to land on the tops of buildings but instead were required to land at one of the heliports in the city. They landed on the East 30th Street heliport and then got into a chauffeured car to Headquarters on Madison Avenue, just near Grand Central Station.

At HQ, they descended to Yellow Level and Turnkey and Al debriefed the leadership. The U.S.A. began an intense research effort on Moon International. Their top priority was to find Dr. Zerick Moonshae and Al's parents.

The Alexandrian Lamp made its way to Mary-Anne's lab on Blue Level. She and Tee began an analysis immediately. What secrets the lamp held would soon be unveiled.

Al was brought into the Chief's office for a private meeting.

The Chief sighed. "Agent Dangermond. Your efforts to recover the Serpent's Blade may have been warranted and courageous, but the result is failure."

"What? Seriously, Chief, after all of that?"

Nothing good ever happened to him in the Chief's office.

The Chief looked right at Al. "Correct. You didn't retrieve the sword. That was your mission and you failed."

"But sir, I found out more. That has to count for something."

"Yes, Agent Dangermond, of course it counts for something. But my friend, Mr. Fudosan, can't know any of the details of this interesting development you've discovered.

The information is classified and we have no sword to give back to him. I'm upgrading your field rating from Gamma to Beta, but I can't mark the mission as a success.

"Well, that's ridiculous," Al said, softly.

"Ridiculous or not, Agent, that is the truth. Until you recover the sword, the mission will be checked-off as incomplete."

Al couldn't appreciate the Chief's position. The Chief even got on his case about the email and the video that he had hidden from the agency that Moonshae had sent. Al thought he had done a good job, but apparently the Chief was dissatisfied with the result.

~

Al shrugged his shoulders. "I don't know what he wants, TK. I mean we've uncovered something big here."

Turnkey put a hand on Al's shoulder. "Yo, homie, don't let him get you down. He's just being the Chief. Did he say anything else?"

Alabaster nodded his head as he sat down in the chair of their shared bedroom. "Yeah. He told me more about my parents' trust. He said my trust includes a house in Newport, Rhode Island."

"The one you grew up in? That brown one you told me about?"

"Nah. The Chief said the trust includes a large mansion in Newport that my parents owned. He said one of my relatives made a bunch of money in geology and put it in a will for my dad. My parents transferred it to the trust, and now it's mine."

Turnkey whistled. "And the Chief oversees the trust?

"Yep, until I'm sixteen."

"Or until we rescue your parents." Turnkey stuck out his fist toward Al and the other teen double-bumped it.

Al looked at his partner. "The Chief is sending us to Newport to see if we can find the stone in the large mansion—my mansion." Al chuckled.

41

Evil Machines

Dr. Zerick Moonshae stood in his library looking at the Serpent's Blade. Around him were shelves extending to the top of the ornate room. Rising well over three stories tall and the length of the south wing of the house, the book room featured many sitting areas, scrolling ladders to reach the highest books, more than one hidden door, and a spiral-iron staircase that wound its way to the second and third floors of shelves. On the ceiling was something very special, a painting that spanned the room.

It was a 600-year-old ceiling painting from the old world—old world Italy, and it showed the sky and clouds and little angels floating around in the corners. It was brought to its current location many decades before when the Italian mansion was too old to fix and had to be demolished.

The whole ceiling of the original Italian mansion library was moved as one large piece from Italy and installed in the Moonshae library. The cost in money for the move was enormous, but it was a pittance for a wealthy man like Moonshae.

He compared the etchings on the blade with the writing on the map. Fourteen years ago, he first came across the map deep in the bowels of the Bodleian Library at Oxford University. Zerick had discovered a secret entrance to the special underground Oxford library, snuck in, and stolen the map from the collection. Well, permanently *borrowed*, was how he liked to think of it. Now it had joined many old volumes long forgotten by the world in Moonshae's stacks.

The man looked up at the little angels gazing down on him and smiled. Fortune had once again gone his way. All the years of consuming knowledge in book after book after book were ready to thrust him where no person had ever been before. He had already performed an x-ray of the blade and seen the hidden stone in the handle, Zerick Moonshae felt more content than he had in a decade, but his thirst for more stones remained unquenched. Olaf was smart to scatter them around the world, separated by distance. Their power was nothing so far apart, but united...

The door creaked open and a young man walked in.

"Ah, Cy. How are the preparations for my machine? Have you finished the network configuration?"

"The work is almost complete, Dr. Moonshae. Soon we can begin the tests."

"Good. Very good."

Even though Cy was in Moonshae's inner circle and trusted like Willoughby, Zerick had kept his real name a secret even from him. Moonshae had let that name go many years ago, when he decided to call himself *Dr. Moonshae*. His wealth and knowledge fooled everyone, so no one ever questioned his real name or if he held an advanced degree. It mattered not that he had no PhD, because he had never met anyone who could rival his knowledge.

Moonshae stroked his chin. "Yes, Cy. Very good, indeed," he said. "Go and continue your work."

Cy left the room. Zerick moved over to the wall and pushed a button. A panel opened to reveal a large flat-screen television hidden behind it. The screen came on and he watched his scientists at work. They were prepping the Dangermond couple for a thaw out of cryofreeze. He knew the virtue of mercy was important, but even in all his brilliance, he did not give a second thought to violence if it gained him knowledge.

He grinned at the screen. "Oh yes, young Alabaster. You will give me what I want. And then I will have everything."

~

MANHATTAN, NEW YORK CITY
40.754652 N, 73.978190 W

Al and Turnkey were itching to get back into the field to find Moonshae. But the Chief wanted them to take the night off. He even sprang for tickets to see a baseball game that night before they would go to Newport. The Astros were in town playing the hometown Yankees. Before heading out to catch the game, they met with Mary-Anne in her lab to give her the details on how her gadgets and weapons performed during the mission.

Of course, they had great things to say, since her work had saved their lives on more than one occasion. They even told her about the interesting use of the Impact Suit on top of Katya's building.

"Oh. I'll have to fix that." She made a meticulous note on a scratch pad. "Anything else?" The guys looked at each other and shrugged their shoulders. Al started grinning. "Maybe it would be cool if we had an electro-grenade?" Turnkey nodded vigorously.

As Alabaster looked around the lab at all the new gadgets Mary-Anne was working on, he couldn't help but notice what was sitting in the back of the large laboratory.

"Hey, that's my motorcycle!" he said, pointing to the sleek black bike that had some damage on the side from hitting Katya's apartment building. Turnkey and Mary-Anne followed him to the two motorcycles.

Al smiled as he ran his hand on the bike. "These bikes are sport'n. You've really outdone yourself."

The brown-haired girl smiled, looking at the machines. "Thanks, Al. It was fun to build them. I keep thinking of all kinds of new gadgets to put onboard."

She pressed a series of buttons on Turnkey's motorcycle.

"Hmm…" Mary-Anne gave a little giggle. "Say, guys.

I think you forgot one of my really important gadgets on the mission." A thin compartment opened on the side of the motorcycle.

She pointed. "I put this secret space in the bike just for you, Turnkey. Just press the edge."

He peered into the compartment and pressed the edge. Out popped a tray with a bundle wrapped in a space-age vacuum pack.

He picked up the pack. "Ouch! It's hot!"

"Of course it is, silly. I don't short-change my agents."

Turnkey opened the package and gave everyone a hot homemade cookie. "You're the best, Mary-Anne." Everyone laughed as they bit into those delicious sweet morsels.

Tomorrow they would begin their manhunt for Dr. Zerick Moonshae and the recovery of the Serpent's Blade—and maybe, just maybe, Alabaster Dangermond's parents.

Just the beginning.

Look for the continuation of this story in
Alabaster Dangermond and Astrid's Jewel.

Want more Alabaster Dangermond?

Join Al, Turnkey, & Mary-Anne online at
alabasterdangermond.com

Get exclusive content on Agent Missions
Sneak-peeks at upcoming books
Behind the scenes on the Dangermond Series
Book cover reveals
Author news & more!

Acknowledgments

At tuck-in time, when my children were very little, Alabaster Dangermond came to life. One night they asked me to tell them an adventure story and I created Al and his friends. Soon, the serious worldbuilding began when my kids requested more details of Al and Turnkey as they faced off against their archnemesis, Dr. Zerick Moonshae. What started as a bedtime routine turned into a weekly telling of new missions whenever we were in the car. "Dad, tell us another Alabaster Dangermond story," my kids would say. Encouraged by them and my wife, I began to write down the various mission details and from there, I began to write with serious intent.

I want to thank my family, friends, and professional colleagues for their encouragement, eye for critique toward improvement, and for their generous love of literature and writing. I want to thank God for the opportunity to write this story and say to the love of my life, Kellie, thank you for making this possible.

Dr. Jason VanHorn is a professor of geography. Fascinated by the interwoven fabric of people and places around the world, he loves to think about geographical interactions. Interested in security, secret intelligence, and spies, he loves to write both fiction and non-fiction. When he is not writing, you can find him throwing a baseball, camping, playing video games with his kids, or hanging out on social media. He started writing at an early age and had dreams in high school of one day completing a novel. Alabaster Dangermond and the Serpent's Blade is his first novel.

CPSIA information can be obtained
at www.ICGtesting.com
Printed in the USA
BVHW03s1118130318
510150BV00001BA/16/P